Out of the Shadows

Love, Lies & Consequences Book IV

NATASHA D. FRAZIER

Also by Natasha D. Frazier

<u>Devotionals</u>

The Life Your Spirit Craves

Not Without You

The Life Your Spirit Craves for Mommies

Not Without You Prayer Journal

<u>Fiction</u>

Love, Lies & Consequences

Through Thick & Thin: Love, Lies & Consequences Book 2

Shattered Vows: Love, Lies & Consequences Book 3

Kairos: The Perfect Time for Love

<u>Non-fiction</u>

How Long Are You Going to Wait?

Note from the Author

Wow! Book #10! When I published my first book in 2012, I had no idea where it would lead. This journey has been amazing and I'm thankful that God has allowed me to pursue my dream and that He has connected me to readers like you who continue to support me.

God has given me a wonderful family who supports my writing career. Eddie, my awesome husband, I love you and appreciate you for all that you do. Thank you for your unwavering support. My babies: Eden, Ethan & Emilyn, mommy loves each of you dearly. To my mom, dad, stepdad and sisters, I thank you for your love and support. For my sister Courtney who doesn't want to be lumped in with everyone else, I love you and thank you for your support.

To my special set of girlfriends who push me to go further and have encouraged me from the very start: Tiera, Toccara & Shenitra - I love you ladies and appreciate your friendship. Nichole is Team Love, Lies & Consequences all the way and I am forever thankful for you my sister! I consider myself blessed to be surrounded by such an awesome group of women.

Readers - Thank you for continuing on this literary journey with me. You each hold a special place in my heart, so please know that with every stroke of the keyboard, I am thinking of you, seriously. When I began writing this book, all I knew is that Chloe had to have a better ending than what she had in Book 3 and this book totally morphed into something special. I hope that you'll find some of the lessons that our characters learn to heart and be blessed by them. Enjoy! To the 5aithful 5abulous 5ive book club, Joy & Company, Miss Ella of EDC Creations, BRAB, and many other book clubs and readers who help get the word out and have shown tremendous support, my heart swells with gratitude. Thank you!

Much love & many blessings,

Natasha

Chapter 1

"Five, four, three, two, one! Happy New Year!" Shane and Chloe shouted along with the rest of the congregation. There was hardly a dry eye in the building as the congregation reflected on Pastor's sermon and shared hugs and high fives with one another—grateful to have made it into the New Year. The choir emotionally sang, "You Made a Way" while the congregation celebrated. Pastor Jacobs had just finished his sermon, titled "Kneel Before You Build," encouraging parishioners to seek God before creating their New Year goals.

"No more resolutions because resolutions tend to get tossed to the side after mid-February. Uh-uh, I won't get any Amens on that. This year, I want each of you to be people of faith. Be intentional about the path that you're going to take. Set your goals after being led by our Lord. And then take it a step further and create a plan to accomplish those goals. Faith without works is dead—isn't that right, church?" Pastor Jacobs preached. He went on to encourage his members to bring their plans to church at the end of the month so that he could pray over them.

Shane wondered what was in store for him and Chloe. It had been a little over a year since Rico passed away. To Shane's dismay, he and Chloe were still only *friends.* He knew she needed time to grieve her late husband, no matter how he had treated her, but Shane was ready for her to move on—with him. He didn't want to keep bringing up the situation for fear that Chloe might feel like he was rushing her, but what was he to do? Wait forever? He would move on if someone else even compared to her, but he didn't believe such a woman existed.

"What are your plans for this year?" Shane asked during the ride home. She had seemed pretty emotional during the service and all he could do was provide hugs, prayers, and an occasional squeeze of the hand.

"Hopefully something greater than my past. Honestly, other than tonight, I haven't prayed about or thought about it much. What about you?"

Other than taking things a step forward with you? Shane wanted to ask, but instead he answered, "I want to try something different in the force. Something more like a desk job, you know? I'm getting a little older, so I want to settle down. No more chasing bad guys. I've been praying that God would provide opportunities for that to happen. So when you think about me, add that to your prayer list." There were only so many ways that he could tell her that he was ready, and this was yet another way of showing her. He didn't need her worrying about him too much while he was at work. She'd told him once that she couldn't live with the thought of knowing he may not come home at night because of his line of work. Now it was something he was ready to change.

"Of course! That's great Shane. That'll be a great move for you."

Shane nodded in agreement.

When he pulled into her driveway, he shut the engine off and for a moment it was silent. He searched for the right words to help her see that they were right for each other and the time was now, or at least soon, for them to decide if their relationship was ever going to go any further.

"Please be patient with me," Chloe said as if she could hear Shane's thoughts. "I know you've been doing that, but just give me a little more time."

Shane nodded slowly, not sure what direction the conversation was headed. He'd been there for her, just like he said he would. He'd been around to cheer her up, take her out to brighten her spirits, and give her a shoulder to cry on. If she just needed someone to sit with her, he was that person. He wouldn't change any of that, because he loved her and wanted to be the person she trusted and relied upon. He just wished that she could see that would never change and that was who he'd always be to her—whatever she needed him to be.

"You've been so amazing to me. I guess what I'm trying to say is my hesitation has nothing to do with you. You know how much I went through; I just want to be sure that I can be the woman you need me to be before we take our relationship further. You need me to be whole," Chloe said, reaching over to caress his hand.

"I can understand that. I won't push too hard," he said and chuckled softly. His face turned serious before he continued, "But I'm ready . . . lady, I've been ready most of my life."

"I see that now." Chloe leaned over and planted a kiss on his cheek. She was grateful for the friend she had in Shane.

"I won't keep you any longer. It's very late."

After Shane saw her safely inside, he revved up his engine and drove home, but sat in his driveway for a while, thinking about the conversation he'd just had with Chloe. Years ago he had come to the realization that he and Chloe would never be together, when she grew up and gave her heart to someone else. When she returned home with the news that she was getting a divorce, his hopes were raised, but they were quickly let down again when she told him that her ex-husband was dying and that she would be devoted to her husband until the very end, no matter what had previously gone on between them. And that left him right where he was now . . . waiting for her to accept him and his love in a way that would lead to their forever.

Chapter 2

New Year's Day was far from ordinary for the McKinneys. Raegan and Caleb rang it in in Florida with Raegan's parents. Unfortunately, their visit wasn't purely for the sake of spending time with family. Raegan's father had coronary artery disease and had recently suffered a mild heart attack. They'd hoped that spending time with her grandbabies would help ease her mother's worries.

Eric, her brother, was a soldier with the third infantry division in Fort Benning, Georgia. He'd planned to spend the holidays with them, but his plans were cancelled when he received notice of deployment. Raegan understood and was grateful for his service, but hated that she didn't get to see him outside of a computer or phone screen. If he wasn't in battle, then he was doing field training exercises preparing for one. But that was his job; he'd been an infantry soldier since he enlisted in the army while in college. While his family was waiting for him to decide on a major, Eric surprised them all by joining the army.

Raegan spent the morning giving her parents' attic a much needed cleaning. Elbows deep in boxes, Raegan came across pictures of her parents when they were younger and baby pictures of her and her brother. As she continued to mull through the pictures, she noticed that her mother wasn't present in any of her infant pictures, only her father. She thought it strange, but figured her mom didn't want the camera to capture her post-partum body or maybe her mother was simply always the one holding the camera. Her father was grinning from ear to ear in every single photo of the two of them. His smile was contagious and she reflected that same smile as she looked at picture after picture of the two of them.

She paused when she came across one photo of another woman holding her. There was something familiar about the woman's face, but she was quite certain she didn't know her. She put the picture aside to ask her parents about it later. She'd been sitting in the attic thumbing through old pictures for so long that Caleb came to check on her. She heard the creaking of the ladder and the sound of his voice moments before his head appeared through the opening.

"You all right up here babe? We're all starting to worry about you. Cassie and Caleb Jr. have started whining for you."

"Well that makes me feel special, I think. The plan was to come up here and organize some of this stuff for Momma, but I got a little sidetracked when I found a box of old pictures."

"Trying to do away with the snaggle-tooth, pigtailed Raegan Camille? No worries. You know I love you no matter what," Caleb teased.

"Ha ha. Very funny," she said sarcastically and pulled the photo from her back pocket and handed it to Caleb. He glanced at it, handed it back to her, and shrugged his shoulders, unsure of the significance.

"That's not Momma. Did you notice?"

"Yeah. And?"

"My momma isn't in any baby pictures that I saw of me. At least not in any of the earlier ones. I was probably about one when I started seeing her in any of the pictures."

"What are you implying?" Caleb asked, taking the picture from Raegan to look at the woman again. The longer Caleb inspected the photograph, the more he noticed that she and Raegan had similar features. He didn't think that he'd ever met her though.

"Nothing. Just makes me wonder what was going on back then. I'm going to ask my parents about it later."

"Well it's time for a break anyway. Come on down for dinner."

Raegan leaned forward on all fours and kissed Caleb, who never left the steps. Satisfied that she was leaving the attic, he made his way down, holding the ladder to help her to the floor. Raegan grabbed hold of his hand and followed him downstairs into the kitchen. Everyone seemed to have been waiting on the two of them. She kissed her mom, dad, and the kids, and walked over to the sink to wash her hands.

Washing her hands took longer than usual as her eyes adjusted to the light and her thoughts swiveled around the pictures she'd been thumbing through for the last hour. The light in the attic was much dimmer. She wasn't sure she was prepared for the answers she'd be given if she started with the line of questioning. But she needed confirmation of what she was thinking, that pictures of her and her mom had been destroyed or lost. That had to be it.

Her father looked at her when she joined them at the table. "I know the attic is a little dusty, but you've been scrubbing like you're about to perform a surgery. Are you all right, my dear?"

"I think so," she answered and darted her eyes from her father to Caleb, who smiled, signaling that he supported her no matter what. His smile encouraged her, so she took a deep breath and told her father about the pictures. She wasn't sure what kind of response she was expecting from him, but braced herself for the worst.

"Daddy," she began and took a deep breath before continuing. Everything within her danced as she mustered the courage to talk about what she'd seen, or rather, didn't see. "I came across quite a few of my baby pictures while I was in the attic and I noticed that Momma wasn't in most of them, especially when I was a newborn. What happened to those pictures? Did you all lose them or were they damaged by water or fire or something?" she asked, attempting to answer her own question.

"What do you mean? There are plenty of pictures in here of you and your mother." Breaking eye contact, he moved around her to wash his hands before taking a seat across from his wife, Marlena.

"Who is this?" Raegan asked, pulling the picture from her back pocket and placing it on the table. She hesitantly pushed it in front of her mother and father and sat down.

"Okay, we'll go in the living room for a bit to give you all a few minutes," Caleb announced, excusing himself and whisking Cassie, Caleb Jr., and Nicholas away from the dinner table while Raegan and her parents talked.

Marlena mouthed *tell her*. They thought they had been more careful and put away anything that would cause Raegan to question who she was. Even though Raegan was in her thirties, now still didn't seem to be a right time to tell her.

"Marlena is not your biological mother."

Chapter 3

Raegan's body stiffened at the revelation, and for several minutes, she hardly blinked and didn't speak. What did all of this mean? How was any of this even possible? Didn't she look like Marlena? Didn't she act and sound like her? Didn't people say they were cut from the same cloth? What was this? Her mind raced in an effort to make sense of the fact that her mother was not her mother. She slowly turned to look at Caleb, who had been trying to keep their children occupied in the next room and still hear what was going on in the kitchen.

"It's okay, honey. Take a minute to process the information and think before you speak. A gentle answer turns away wrath, but a harsh word stirs up anger," he quoted Scripture before turning his attention back to the children who were playing with blocks and balls, making a mess of the living space that Marlena straightened moments before they moved into the kitchen for dinner.

Raegan blinked back tears and turned her attention away from him as if he'd been speaking a foreign language, and turned back to her parents, who had said nothing since her father broke the news.

"Raegan, honey, you are my daughter as far as I'm concerned, and I've loved you ever since the moment I laid eyes on you," her mother attempted to ease the blow.

Raegan remained silent. She looked from her parents, to Caleb standing in the doorway. Apparently everyone thought it was okay to lie to her all of her life, but this was clearly unacceptable. So if her mother wasn't her mother, then who was? And how did all of this happen? She slid away from the dinner table and made her way through the living room to the front door, where she stopped in her tracks at Cassie's wailing. She did her best to console and reassure her that she would return. She picked her up and rocked her for a couple of minutes, before putting her in Caleb's arms. She had to get out of that house. She hurried out the door to the sidewalk and started her trek down the street. She didn't know how long she'd be gone or where the path would lead; she would walk until something made sense or she could make the pain go away, whichever came first.

Caleb left the children in Marlena and Robert's care and rushed out behind her yelling for her to stop, but she continued walking without looking back. Caleb jogged until he caught up with her and attempted to get her to come back inside.

"Cami, hold on a minute!"

"Babe, I just really need a moment to myself. Take care of the babies; they need you right now."

"They need *us*," Caleb corrected.

Raegan continued walking with her arms folded, hoping that Caleb would back off for a moment and give her the space she needed. She admired his resolve to take care of her, pursue her, and calm her, but she didn't really want that right now. She wanted space, and Caleb refused to give it to her. After news like that, he couldn't and wouldn't leave her alone.

"I'm not leaving you. I'll allow you to think, but I will be right by your side as you do so."

Raegan agreed, but she didn't say so; she only shrugged and continued to walk. She was not going to talk. Besides, she didn't have the words to say. She wasn't even sure she knew who she was anymore.

"Just let me be here for you," Caleb said, reaching for her hand that was tucked away under her arm. She relented and gave him her hand, but remained quiet as she allowed her thoughts to take control. Caleb prayed silently as they walked. Since his wife refused to talk to him, he chose to go to God, who could guide them in this difficult time.

Back in the house, Raegan's mother and father fed and entertained the children while Raegan and Caleb were away.

"She's taking it pretty hard, Robert. What are we going to do about it?" Marlena asked as they moved Nicholas and the twins back into the living room to give them a little more freedom to play.

"I don't know. But she is a strong woman. You did a great job raising her. She'll come around."

"*We* did a great job. But you know what the next question is going to be, right? She's gonna want to know the circumstances surrounding her adoption and what happened to her birth mother." Marlena spoke softly so that the kids couldn't hear her, though the children were too young to understand what was happening.

"That's the part that's going to hurt the most, and that's what concerns me."

"I miss this," Marlena said. "The innocence of children. Their only worries were what to play with next. Their unwavering trust and love." She sighed as she thought about how they were going to have to rebuild all of that with Raegan.

"Don't worry dear. We'll all heal from this," Robert encouraged as he rolled the ball to Nicholas.

When they arrived back at her parents' home, Raegan stopped. Although she felt a little better, pain was awaiting her on the other side of the door. There was no running from this situation. She had to learn the truth, whether she really wanted to or not.

"What do you need me to do, sweetheart?"

"Pray, because I don't know what's on the other side of this or even how to handle it."

Caleb took her hands into his and began praying, right in the middle of the sidewalk where they stood.

"Heavenly Father, we want to thank You for being who You are and Your faithfulness to us. We believe that You will never leave us nor forsake us, and that Your presence is always with us. Right now, we want to lift up my wife to You. Give her comfort and understanding. Be her guide as she seeks to make sense of what's happening in her life. And most of all, help her to maintain a spirit of love, no matter what lies ahead. In Jesus' name we pray, Amen."

Chapter 4

Chloe fought the covers, getting them all twisted around her body as she lamented the most recent excuse she'd given Shane—*I need to be whole.* It's not like she was half of a person, but the last year of her life left her unsure about a lot of things. The confident woman she'd become got lost somewhere between the divorce proceedings and death of Rico, coupled with her move back to Nashville. She wanted and needed to start over; she just wasn't sure how to do that. Because she couldn't quite find her way, she didn't know how to express that to Shane in a way that made sense. She was still trying to make sense of it herself.

The doorbell chimed, causing her to wrestle with the covers even more so she could get out of bed. That was likely her sister, Kelly, on the other side of the door. With the kids at her parents', they planned to do their New Year's Day shopping at Dillard's. Chloe tumbled out of bed and raced to the door, not realizing that she'd overslept.

"Why aren't you ready? We're gonna miss the good stuff!"

"Happy New Year to you too, sis!" Chloe tossed over her shoulder after opening the door. She headed back to her bedroom to dress quickly for their shopping trip.

"I already texted you Happy New Year!" Kelly retorted to Chloe's retreating back while heading toward the refrigerator to find a quick bite for breakfast. At this rate, stopping for something on the way was out of the question.

Chloe emerged ten minutes later, dressed in a pair of blue jeans and a green sweater. She brushed her short hair flat, washed her face and brushed her teeth, before slipping into the first clothes she saw. Chloe was convinced that having kids turned Kelly into a drill sergeant when it came to keeping time. Surprisingly, she didn't call beforehand.

Kelly dropped a couple of Pop Tarts in the toaster oven, leaned against the counter with her arms folded across her chest, and turned to watch Chloe move about the kitchen grabbing orange juice from the fridge and glasses from the cupboard. Chloe poured a glass for each of them before challenging Kelly.

"Are you just going to stand there and burn a hole through my head with your eyes, or do you have something to say, missy?"

"Hmph." The toaster dinged and she grabbed her Pop Tarts, put them in a paper towel, stopped at the table to drink her juice, and started toward the door. "Time is ticking. Let's roll."

Chloe rolled her eyes and returned the juice carton to the refrigerator before trailing Kelly to the car. As nosey as Kelly had always been, Chloe hated when she bit her tongue. She expected nothing less than to hear what Kelly was thinking, whether she wanted to know or not.

"What is that all about?" Chloe asked after making herself comfortable in the passenger seat.

"Nothing. It's a new year. Just waiting to hear the news about you and Shane. You do have news don't you?"

Chloe wondered if *matchmaker* was Kelly's middle name. Shane had won Kelly over shortly after Chloe moved back to town. She agreed that Chloe needed time to grieve her marriage and the death of Rico, but the last thing she wanted Chloe to do was fall into depression. She couldn't tell her when it was time to move on, but Chloe deserved some happiness and Shane was ready and more than willing to play his role in it.

"I don't expect you or anyone else to understand," Chloe said.

"Try me."

"Shouldn't you be driving? I thought you were in a rush to get to the sale?"

Kelly started the car and backed out of Chloe's driveway, encouraging her to share what was on her mind.

"I question whether I made the right choice marrying Rico. Sure, I prayed about it, but did I really wait for an answer? I was so ready to get letters before and after my name, MRS and RN, that when the opportunity presented itself, I jumped with little hesitation. And look where I ended up—back where I started."

Kelly nodded for Chloe to continue.

Chloe wanted to make sure that she didn't do the same thing with Shane. If their relationship was pleasing to God and what God wanted for her life, then she would be more than happy to take the next step with Shane. She couldn't afford another heartache. Though she'd attended church at every opportunity, she needed more; she needed to become reacquainted with her heavenly Father. Through everything that had been going on, she continued to pray, but something was missing. And that something was an intimate relationship with her Lord. There was no way she could go anywhere with Shane or with anyone else until she got that in order. After explaining that to Kelly, contrary to what she expected, Kelly understood.

"Sounds like you're taking the first step. You realize that you need to be closer to God. I would certainly encourage you to do that before linking up with any man. I'm always in prayer for you, and you know I just want you healthy and happy, big sis."

Chloe pinched Kelly's cheeks. "Thanks honey bun."

"Stop it! I'm driving . . . why didn't you say anything about this before?"

"I don't know. A little ashamed maybe. I expect me to be farther along spiritually, and I guess I project that onto the rest of you all too."

"Everyone's walk is different. Right? I can't judge you like that. Your relationship with God is personal. I'm just glad to hear that you're putting it first."

"It's about time." *It is about time,* Chloe's conscience echoed. The fact that she'd committed to her spiritual growth brought her some peace, something that had been absent for the past few months. *Come near to God and He will come near to you,* James 4:8, came to her mind. As Kelly whipped her car into a parking space at Dillard's, all Chloe could think about was the date she had that evening with her heavenly Father.

Chapter 5

Raegan's movements were robotic as if crossing the threshold back into her parents' home set her on automation. She remained silent as she walked through their home, managing to pick up the twins and carry them off to the guest bedroom for a nap. Caleb followed behind her with Nicholas, who protested along the way, trying to wiggle out of his father's grasp to continue the game he was playing with his grandfather.

They sang, rocked, bounced, and sang some more until all the children were asleep. Tiptoeing out of the bedroom, Raegan led the way back into the family room where her parents remained sitting.

"Okay, tell me everything. I'm ready," Raegan said as she took a seat across from them on the loveseat. She fought back tears at the thought of her entire life being a farce. The family portrait hanging on the wall seemed to taunt her. *Not your real family.* Caleb took a seat next to her and engulfed her hands in his. The comfort of his presence calmed her jittery hands and heart. "From the beginning," Raegan urged.

This was a conversation that Robert was hoping he'd never have to have, but Raegan was a grown woman now, and since she wanted to know the truth, he would give it to her.

"When your aunt Joceyln was in college, she gave tennis lessons to this woman named Cynthia Harrison. Now Cynthia was married, so it was never my intention to see her romantically; it just happened. I'd see her with Jocelyn and we'd talk tennis and I'd offer advice. Then when Jocelyn couldn't work with her, I'd step in. Eventually, we started seeing each other without Jocelyn. We fell in love and she conceived you. I was convinced that she would leave her husband at that time, but no way. She was 'committed and only passing the time with me,'" Robert recalled. He blinked back tears as he rehashed the story, one that he'd put behind him since marrying Marlena.

Raegan's stomach turned and she rocked back and forth as she listened to her father. She didn't like where this story was headed, but she wanted the truth. She needed it, so that she could move on.

"Her husband was in grad school and getting ready to graduate. She wanted to have an abortion, but I refused to let that happen. I convinced her to see the pregnancy through to the end and I would raise you without her, and she could move on with her life and go back to her husband. When she was released from the hospital, I took you and she went on with her business. I haven't spoken with her since. I left Nashville and moved to Florida, and I've been here since. This is where I met your mother, Marlena. All Cynthia did was birth you! Your mother is sitting right here as far as I'm concerned," Robert said sternly, ending the conversation by leaving the family room and heading into the kitchen.

Glancing from Robert's retreating back to a stunned Raegan, Marlena asked, "Are you okay honey? I know that was a lot to take in."

Raegan wasn't sure how she felt. On one hand, Cynthia wanted to end Raegan's life to keep her marriage; and on the other hand, the woman who raised her was sitting across from her with open arms, ready to console her. Caleb took one look at Raegan and advanced toward the powder room to grab tissues. Tears streamed down her face at what she had heard. Should she find Cynthia to show her what she missed out on?

Caleb returned and gently wiped the tears from her cheeks as he handed her a glass of water.

"Thank you babe. I'm okay," she said and returned the glass to him after taking a sip.

Back in the kitchen, Caleb found Raegan's father hunched over the sink, staring out the window, as if he was looking for answers.

"Are you all right, Dad? I know that must have been hard for you too."

"I'm fine. I always have been. Raegan being in my life has brought me joy that she'll never understand. She'll always be my baby girl. I just wish it didn't matter who Cynthia was or what she'd done. But I know better. Raegan is gonna want to find her. No doubt about it," Robert answered. He continued staring out the window, never turning to face Caleb. Robert concealed the truth from Raegan even as an adult because he didn't want her to question whether she'd become like her mother; neither did he want her to go looking for her. When he decided to raise her, they were supposed to be out of Cynthia's life forever. That was the agreement. That was well over thirty years ago now, but knowing Raegan, she wasn't going to let it go until she got the answers she sought.

"She's got me. I'll do my best to help her through it. So don't worry too much. She's stubborn, but she'll come around," Caleb said and gave Robert a few encouraging taps on the shoulder before rejoining Raegan and Marlena in the family room, where it appeared that nothing had transpired. Raegan had yet to say much of anything, and Marlena didn't want to push her.

"Mom, I'm fine. Thanks for everything you've done for me," Raegan said finally.

"It has been my joy and you know that," Marlena answered and moved next to Raegan on the sofa. "It's no different than you raising little Nicholas. Just as easy as it is for you to love him, it was the same for me. I mean, loving and raising you has been more than a pleasure for me and I wouldn't change anything. You hear me?" Marlena assured her, wrapped one arm around her shoulder, and kissed her forehead.

"Thanks Momma, I know." Raegan returned the hug and then sought her father in the kitchen.

"Daddy, I love you," she said and threw her arms around his neck.

"I love you more sweetheart."

"I know that wasn't easy for you, but I'm glad we got everything out in the open."

Her father didn't respond, but tightened his embrace in agreement. The fact that he could have missed the opportunity to raise her dawned on him. Though he hated what Cynthia did to the two of them, he was grateful for the opportunity to be a full-time father to Raegan. And he couldn't thank Cynthia enough for that, so in his mind, maybe they were even. She got to work things out with her husband and he got the chance to experience the joys of fatherhood.

Though Raegan understood perfectly well the love her mother had for her, she couldn't understand how Cynthia could detach herself, especially after feeling the flutters in her womb and experiencing labor and childbirth. Raegan couldn't fathom the disconnect. The best part of her wanted to leave the situation alone and continue to live life as before, but would life ever be the same for her knowing what she knows now?

Chapter 6

Huddled around the breakroom getting his fill of coffee and donuts, Shane welcomed the camaraderie with his fellow officers on his first day back to work in the new year. Before starting on the force, he swore he wouldn't get swept into the donut-and-coffee stereotype, but it was hard not to. Donuts and coffee seemed to be made for each other like grits and eggs or hamburgers and French fries—each good on its own but together even better. Though he didn't indulge regularly, every now and again he had to get his fill of them.

"How's the family, Regina?" Shane asked. Regina and Shane met in the police academy. She was given a hard time by most of the male officers until she proved she could hold her own, but Shane had taken an instant liking to her and they'd been friends since. Shane had always thought her brave to take a job on the force with two young children at home.

"Husband and kids are fine. I enjoyed my time off as much as can be expected with dinosaurs roaring and dolls singing around the house. A few days of that and I couldn't wait to get back in here to save myself."

"Tell me about it. I'm dreaming about the songs sung by that teddy bear that we bought Maya for Christmas. I'm glad she's happy with it, but I'm looking forward to the batteries dying on that thing," Matt added.

Shane chuckled along with Regina and Matt, but he couldn't relate. He could only hope that one day he'd have stories like that to tell.

"So what's up with you and your girl that moved back to town?" Regina turned the attention to Shane.

"McDaniels! My office in five," Captain Ross interrupted before Shane could answer. Captain Ross always got straight to the point, so the lack of new year wishes or idle chatter didn't surprise them. When he spoke, it was always business. Shane was grateful for the interruption, because he didn't have any idea what was going on with him and Chloe, yet Captain Ross popping into the break room summoning him to his office didn't seem like it was a good thing either.

"All right guys, I'll get with you later. Let me see what Ross needs."

"Cool, later man."

"Good luck."

Shane finished off his coffee and tossed the disposable cup in the trash. *What could Ross want with me?* he wondered as he strode toward Captain Ross's office, nodding greetings to a few fellow officers along the way.

"Happy New Year, sir!" Shane greeted Captain Ross when he stepped into his office.

Captain Ross nodded and tossed a file toward Shane.

"DeMarcos is retiring in a few weeks, so this is your shot McDaniels. You take the detective exam next week. If you pass, we'll interview you. Are you sure this is still what you want?" Captain Ross asked, finally tearing his attention away from the file on his desk to look at Shane, assessing him for any sign of uncertainty.

"Absolutely!"

"Good. Test is Monday at ten sharp!"

"Thank you sir!"

"Ten sharp, McDaniels!" Captain Ross dismissed him. No *you're welcome* or *you've earned it,* but Shane wasn't surprised because it seemed that Ross lacked any sort of emotion. No one had ever seen the corners of his mouth turned upward.

Shane tried his best to contain his excitement as he walked out of the precinct to his patrol car. He loved the level of independence he had as a patrol officer, but he was ready for investigations and report writing, among other things. Though being a detective was dangerous too, he hoped that it would give Chloe a little more comfort in knowing that he wasn't out on the streets all day facing danger head on.

But whether she was happy about it or not, he knew that this was the right move for his career. He sat inside his cruiser for a moment looking through the file that Captain Ross handed to him. Everything he needed to know to prepare for the test was included in the file, along with information regarding the pay grade and duties of a detective. He had to share the news with Chloe. This was a special moment for both of them.

"Call CoCo," he commanded.

Calling CoCo.

"Hey there, how are you?" Chloe said upon answering the call.

"I'm great! At the New Year service, I told you that I wanted a desk job, remember?"

"Yeah, I remember that." Chloe was at work, standing around the nurses' station. She excused herself and found an empty room to talk with Shane privately. Though no one knew who she was talking to, she felt like people were judging her for even thinking of moving on with Shane. In reality, the only one who was judging her was herself.

"From my lips to God's ears! I'm taking the detective exam next week!" he yelled with excitement.

"Congratulations! You've got this! I'm so happy for you!" Chloe's voice matched his level of excitement.

"Thank you. I knew you would be." His tone changed from excitement to a more loving and gentle one.

"Let me take you out to celebrate!"

"I'm thinking lobster, shrimp . . . "

"Umm, I was thinking hot dogs, fries, and soda," Chloe said and giggled.

"I was just kidding. Whatever is fine as long as I get to do it with you."

"I heard that. Consider it done."

"So does this mean you're picking me up?" Shane joked. He'd always been the one to drive whenever they went out.

"Sure, when will you be ready?"

"You name the time and I'll be at home gettin' fine."

Chloe giggled. "Whatever. You are so silly. Tonight at seven. See you then."

"I um . . . Okay, bye," Shane ended the call. He almost said *I love you.* Though he did love her and she knew that, they weren't quite ready to be ending their calls with professions of love.

Shane pulled a pen out of his uniform pocket and jotted Philippians 4:13 on the first page in the file handed to him by Captain Ross. That was his reminder that his strength came from God and he was going to do his part to prepare for the exam. He was more than ready for that evening, the next week, and what was to come after. But for now he would focus on getting through the day so that he could get to Chloe that evening. *Be anxious for nothing* erupted from within. Everything would happen in the proper time.

Chapter 7

"You didn't even give me a chance to blow the horn!" Chloe teased when Shane jumped into the passenger seat.

"Nope, I was sitting next to the window peeking out of the blinds for any sign of you."

Chloe laughed at the scene that formulated in her thoughts.

"I kid you not."

"I don't believe it."

"You're right. I had actually just taken out the trash when I saw you down the street, so I went in to grab my coat and lock the door."

"Umm hmm." Chloe leaned toward Shane and tapped her cheek for a kiss.

Shane kissed her cheek but didn't move to settle back into his seat.

"What?"

He tapped his lips just as she had tapped her cheek. She kissed him.

"Now that's more like it CoCo! I haven't seen you in days and all you were going to give me was a one-second peck on the cheek. The least you could give is a two-second peck on the lips."

"Understood Captain," Chloe responded after their kiss. "I think you deserve more than hot dogs and fries. So, where to?"

"Italian sounds good to me right about now."

Shane's restaurant of choice was Molto Bene Ristorante. He'd only been there once in the three years since it opened, but he passed by often while on patrol, so he didn't need to look up directions on his phone. He served as Chloe's GPS by giving her the directions etched in his mind.

The moment Chloe shifted the gear into park, Shane hopped out of the passenger seat and opened the car door for her, extending his arm to help steady her onto the pavement.

Chloe had noticed a valet service out front, but never wanted to use those unless she was alone or there was absolutely no parking available. "This looks nice," she commented as they entered the courtyard and walked along a winding stone path that led to the restaurant entrance.

"It is, but not too fancy. It's fairly casual. The atmosphere reminds me of Olive Garden, but I like the food here much better. I hope you will too."

"I hope so. I'm hungry so I'm not in the mood for sub-par food. I need something really good and satisfying tonight."

"If you don't get what you need, it'll be my pleasure to take you out again to make it up to you."

"I'm sure of it," said Chloe, squeezing his arm a little tighter as they arrived at the hostess station.

"Welcome to Molto Bene. Will it just be the two of you?" the hostess asked.

The restaurant wasn't crowded, so the hostess escorted them to a table immediately. Chloe was impressed by the lighting and the oversized plants. In areas where there would normally be booths in other restaurants, Molto Bene had sofas. The atmosphere was much better than Shane made it out to be. She hoped the food matched the ambience, because she was getting more excited by the second.

"I feel like I should be wearing something a little more fancy being in here," Chloe whispered to Shane after taking their seats.

"You're good. Trust me. You're actually more than good."

"Thanks." Chloe couldn't help but blush. Shane had a way of slathering on the compliments. "So the new year is starting off right for you, huh? I'm so happy for you, Shane. There's nothing like getting exactly what you want."

"I appreciate that. Your support is important to me. You know I'd spoken to Captain about it last month; I just didn't think it would happen so quickly. Either way, it's a great move for me and I'm ready for it."

"So becoming a detective means you'll be off the streets?"

"Sort of. When I'm on the streets, it'll be for different reasons . . . investigating or responding to a crime scene. Everything else will be done from the desk for the most part."

"Yes! That sounds a little safer."

Shane chuckled at her reaction.

"Wait. I sounded too excited about that, huh? Never mind me. This is all about you. So what's good here?" Chloe switched topics.

"I've only had the basil shrimp pasta, and I don't plan on trying anything different tonight."

Chloe nodded and perused the menu. She was indeed enthused about Shane's potential promotion. She wouldn't have to worry about his safety as much, and that would be one less excuse she'd have not to move forward in their relationship. Although what happened with Rico crept into her mind every now and again, that was something she was working through, but she didn't want to live the rest of her life worried every night that he may not come home.

Chloe decided to order the same dish as Shane. After the waiter took their orders and left, Chloe reached into her purse and pulled out a card for Shane.

"You just get sweeter by the day. I'm blessed to have you in my life. You have no idea how much." Shane rose from his seat to thank her with a kiss. "Thank you." When he sat down, he opened the card.

Congratulations on your success! May God continue to guide you along the best path for your life. Commit everything you do unto Him and you will be sure to succeed. With love, Chloe.

"Thank you." Shane thought the card was a nice gesture and he took the handwritten words to heart. He was indeed grateful to have Chloe in his life, and although this move was one that he was doing for himself, he hoped that it would help Chloe decide that a long-term relationship between the two of them could work.

Shane shifted the conversation to Chloe and how things were going at the hospital. She enjoyed her work and her coworkers. Although one coworker seemed to be jealous of her and went out of her way to be rude, she didn't let it bother her, and she didn't mention that to Shane. She missed the coworkers in Houston who had become friends, but they kept in touch through social media. Otherwise she was adjusting well to her new position at Nashville Medical Center.

Dinner arrived and their conversation was cut to a minimum for a short period. Chloe was serious when she said she was hungry and her entrée hit the spot. Not only was it delicious, but the serving was two and a half times as much as she needed. A to-go box was definitely in order.

"That was the best Italian food I've ever had. I needed that."

"So does that mean I don't have to make it up to you by taking you somewhere else?" Shane teased.

"I'm always open for another date, but we don't have to consider it a make-up date. This was amazing," Chloe touted, patting her belly.

Shane agreed, but unlike her, he finished his meal. They declined dessert and Shane scooped up the check, placed his card in the holder and handed it to the waitress with protest from Chloe, causing the waitress to hesitate before leaving their table.

"No, what are you doing? This was my treat to you, Shane."

"I know and I appreciate that, but please allow me to take care of it."

Chloe relented and nodded toward the waitress, who left to close out their check. Shane had always been so kind to her, she wished he would have let her do this for him, but knowing there would be other times, she dismissed the thought.

They walked hand in hand out of the restaurant back to Chloe's car. Always a gentleman, he opened her door and saw her safely inside before letting himself in on the passenger side.

"Thank you for taking me out. I needed to get out since I'm going to spend the next several days making sure I'm ready for this test. I needed this . . . needed to see you."

"I think we both needed it," Chloe agreed. Their gazes lingered on each other before she started the car.

When she arrived at Shane's house, he turned to her and said, "Thank you for trying. I know you've gone through a lot over the past couple of years. I'm not rushing you, but I'm here whenever you're ready. Okay?"

He'd mulled over whether or not he would bring up the idea of them becoming more serious on the ride back from the restaurant, but decided against it. Although he'd mentioned it before, he didn't want her to believe that his career move was to inspire her to take their relationship a little further. He was going to do his best to give her the time she needed to come around.

"I know and I thank you for being patient with me Shane. I have every intention of being with you; I just want to make sure the timing is right. We'll get there. Promise."

Shane responded with a kiss, asked her to call him when she arrived home, and stepped out of the car. He stood outside until he could no longer see her tail lights in the distance. He made a mental note not to let her pick him up anymore. He didn't like the idea of her driving alone late at night. It made him feel better that they were making progress and they would soon be together . . . finally.

Chapter 8

"She knows."

Cynthia's pulse raced quickly at the sound of his voice echoing through the line. Robert Frank Sanders. There hadn't been much communication between her and Robert since she left him and their baby and chose her marriage. Honestly, she thought that part of her would remain hidden from both Chloe and Kelly forever. She thought to tell the entire truth more than a year ago when she divulged she cheated on their father, but thought better of it. Her goal was to encourage Chloe to stay in her marriage and to understand the strength it took to withstand trials, not push her farther away from Rico. Chloe would never forgive her for lying, especially at a time when she needed to hear the truth from those she cared for most.

Now her ugly past had come knocking on the door again, and she was all out of defenses.

"What do you want me to do?" Cynthia's voice trembled as her mind continued to race. What would she say to Chloe and Kelly? It had been more than thirty years, but would this open old wounds for David?

"Be prepared for some type of contact sooner or later."

"Did you give her my number?" Cynthia's voice raised an octave and her stomach twisted in knots. She eased onto a seat on the sofa and wrapped her free arm around her waist as she rocked back and forth.

"Not yet, but you have to know that whether or not I give her your information, Cyn, she's going to find you. She's strong willed and persistent like that . . . just like you."

"I see." Cynthia chewed her bottom lip, something she rarely did because she thought it to be improper, and continued to allow her thoughts to swirl. Robert was talking but she missed everything he said.

"Yes or no?"

"I'm sorry, I missed that. Yes or no to what?"

"Do you want me to give her your number?"

"Let me get back with you on that," Cynthia said before ending the call. That was not the news she was expecting today, or any day for that matter.

She now sat on the edge of the sofa with both arms wrapped around her midsection as she rocked back and forth trying to figure out what she would say to her child whom she'd walked away from—and what she would say to her children who knew nothing about that child? Would they welcome her with open arms? Would they want to have a relationship with her? Would they despise their mother for not telling them the truth at least when they became old enough to possibly understand and accept her choice?

She reached for the Bible on the coffee table and flipped it open for guidance. *What am I doing?* She thought before snapping the Bible shut. She closed her eyes and prayed earnestly for direction. When she finished praying, the word *truth* resonated in her spirit along with Proverbs 12:19, "Truthful lips endure forever, but a lying tongue lasts only a moment." She could quote many Scriptures that spoke to the subject of truth, but reading Proverbs 12:19 at that moment pierced her heart. She knew she could no longer hide the fact that she'd given her daughter up; and knowing that she would soon have to relive the pain and now potentially hurt her family with her lies caused her even more grief. Would Chloe and Kelly forgive her? And how would this affect her husband, David? Cynthia wept and prayed once more, seeking God for guidance to get through a potential tumultuous situation that she'd tried so hard to leave in the past.

Chapter 9

"Cami, do you want me to get us tickets to the comedy show at the Toyota Center for Valentine's Day?" Caleb called to Raegan from the restroom as he brushed his teeth. After a moment with no response from her, he walked back into their master bedroom to find her face glued to the computer screen.

"Sweetheart, did you hear me?"

"Oh, I'm sorry, yeah, sure," she answered, not even certain of what she was agreeing to. Caleb's words didn't register, only his voice. Raegan was busy investigating Cynthia via Google.

Raegan had spent the last month going back and forth regarding whether or not she would reach out to Cynthia. One day she would be all for it and the next she would decide to move on with her life because she had all that she needed. Besides, Marlena had been a great mother to her. Would seeking out Cynthia be a slap in Marlena's face? Would she be offended? Although she'd said she was fine with whatever Raegan decided, was she really?

Raegan had to figure out what she wanted from Cynthia if she were to find her. What would be the purpose of meeting her? Just to hear where her mind was at the time and why she would willingly walk away from her? What would that prove?

What next? Would she be able to move on once she heard her out? Did she want Cynthia to be a part of her life? She developed a headache trying to solve all of her problems with a few strokes of the keyboard.

"I have a feeling that you don't know what you agreed to. What's going on with you? You've been distracted lately," Caleb asked, gently guiding her from the corner desk to their bed. He sat on the floor in front of her and began massaging her feet. "Tell me what's bothering you."

"I've tried, but I just can't seem to get over this whole situation with my birth mother. I think I need to find her."

"I can't imagine what this must be doing to you, but I'd like to help you. What do you need me to do? I'll do anything, because I want my Cami back."

"Is that why you're giving me a foot massage?"

"Nah, foot massages help you relax and that's what I'm trying to help you do—relax."

"I love you, you know that?"

"Sometimes," Caleb answered before letting out a hearty chuckle.

Raegan playfully tagged him with a pillow, causing him to tickle her feet in return before he joined her on the bed. It warmed his heart to see the smile that emanated from her and lit up her features.

Caleb leaned on his elbow and picked up the conversation where it left off. "Tell me what you need me to do."

"Part of me wants to book a ticket to Nashville, because that's where she is, and another part wants me to walk away. I haven't decided."

"What have you found out about her so far?"

"She lives in Nashville and she's married. Not much really, I guess."

Raegan hadn't found much information about Cynthia Harrison on the internet. She didn't seem to have a Facebook account, so that made it harder to find information about her. The most she found was information relating to Cynthia's volunteer work at her church. At least she found a more recent picture of her, so she knew what Cynthia looked like. She could see why her father would fall for someone like her; Cynthia was beautiful.

"Let's not get ahead of ourselves. I don't think it's wise for you to show up without warning and demanding answers. You should at least have a conversation with her and see if she'll even agree to meet with you." Caleb spoke slowly in an effort to choose his words wisely. He didn't want his wife getting her feelings hurt if Cynthia didn't want to see her at all. She had to at least consider that was a possibility given that Cynthia walked away from Raegan in the first place. He hoped to convey that without reminding her that Cynthia abandoned her.

"You're right. Besides, I honestly don't know what I would say to her or even what I hope to gain by meeting her. I'll pray about it before making a decision."

"Uh uh. We'll pray about it. I'm your partner in everything, Cami."

Raegan smiled and nodded in agreement. The couple sat up in the bed, legs folded and touching, and linked hands as Caleb led them in prayer. "Spirit of the living God, we enter into Your presence to say thank You for being who You are in our lives. We believe Your Word that says that You care about even the smallest things in our lives. Lord, You even know the number of hairs on our heads. And because You care so deeply for us, we come casting our cares upon You and asking that You gently guide us when it comes to our approach regarding Cynthia. What would You have us do and how would You have us do it? We thank You for Your faithfulness and we dare not move without You leading us. In Jesus' name, Amen."

"I'm so thankful for you babe. What would I do without you?"

"You'd be sitting around waiting for me to come back in your life again, that's what," Caleb said and chuckled, reminding her of his version of how they reconnected.

Raegan grabbed the pillow and playfully tagged him with it before planting a soft kiss on his lips. Gratefulness flowed through her heart knowing that Caleb loved her so much; and no matter what was next, she knew she could handle it with him by her side.

Chapter 10

Cynthia leaned in closer to the mirror as she applied a little more concealer than usual. She hadn't slept much since her conversation with Robert a week and a half ago. The last time she could remember being so uncomfortable and tossing about throughout the night was during pregnancy. The news he'd given her had shaken her so; all she could think about was whether or not her daughter would seek her out and what Cynthia could say to make her believe that she loved her even though she chose to give her up. Were there any words?

That was one topic that she and David never spoke about. The deed had been done. Was there anything to say? He never once asked her if she thought about her child or whether she regretted her decision. *But why would he?* she mused. She'd given up the baby to save her marriage, or at least that's what she thought she was doing. Giving up her baby to be raised alone by Robert made her heart ache daily, and she tried as much as she could to push it away from her mind.

Once she and David reconciled, she wanted to get pregnant as soon as possible to suppress her guilt of giving up her baby girl. Chloe was her do-over. Her second chance to do everything right.

Rat-a-tat-tat!

David's light taps on the door reeled her mind back from memory lane. She hurriedly dabbed at the few stray tears that had escaped from her eyes as she thought about her past and future.

"Are you all right in there? I thought you said you were almost ready. That was about thirty minutes ago."

"Finishing up my face. I'll be out in less than five minutes," she called out to her husband. In all the time they'd been married, he'd always honored her privacy when she was in the bathroom with the door shut. He'd always told her that he didn't want to walk in on her doing any lady stuff. She was way past menopause, but thankfully, he had become a creature of habit.

"Okay then. I'll just pour your coffee in your thermos and wait for you in the car."

As promised, Cynthia emerged from the bathroom five minutes later, proud of what she'd been able to accomplish on her face. If she didn't know any better, even she'd believe that she was well rested, since she managed to conceal the dark circles under her eyes.

David waited until she was comfortable in her seat, had a few sips of coffee, and they were well into their thirty-minute drive to church before he spoke.

"What's been bothering you, Cyn?"

"Everything is fine," she said, though things were far from fine. The rehearsed phrase slipped from her lips too easily.

She could have told the truth, but she didn't want to deal with it on the way to church. Did he really need that distraction during service?

"I'm not so sure it is." From his experience, every time Cynthia said, "I'm fine," that actually meant that she wasn't okay and something was bothering her. And oftentimes, he became just as uneasy as she until he knew what bothered her and how he could help make it better.

"Why do you say that?"

"After more than thirty years, you think I wouldn't notice if my wife wasn't lying next to me at night? You've been in and out of bed throughout the night for the past week. Something is bothering you, and as your husband I hope that you will allow me to carry some of this burden." He laced his fingers with hers and raised them to his lips. "Let's talk about it later, Cyn. I love you."

She whispered "I love you" in return and thought for a moment. Would it make a difference if they talked about it now or later? Did he really know what he was asking? Was this a burden he was willing to bear? The circumstances surrounding Raegan more than thirty years ago nearly tore them apart and rightfully so. Cynthia sat for a moment trying to come up with any reasonable explanation that would put David at ease, but in the deep recesses of her heart, she knew that only the truth would do.

She opened her mouth to speak but couldn't find the words. How was she supposed to tell him that the child she'd given up more than thirty years ago would likely be standing at their front door sometime soon? She closed her eyes, took a deep breath, and said, "She's looking for me."

"Who?" David was confused. Cynthia always expected him to read her mind. *She* could be anyone, and why would anyone be looking for his wife?

"The baby I gave up over thirty years ago." There. She'd said it. Part of the weight had been lifted from her shoulders, but she didn't know what her confession had done to David. For a long moment, he didn't say anything. He continued to go through the motions of maneuvering the car through traffic to get them to their destination. His features became stiff, and if she didn't know any better, she could have sworn he didn't blink either.

"What is your plan?" He didn't know how to handle the situation. He never spoke about the baby, because he wasn't sure if Cynthia's choice to completely disconnect from the child was the best decision. But at the time he was infuriated. She'd not only broken their vows, but she messed around and got pregnant as well. He was hurt and didn't ever think that he would heal from that pain, but with God's help and a lot of prayer, he did. Keeping the child would have been a constant reminder of her indiscretion because undoubtedly, Robert would want to be a part of the child's life. That was a lose-lose situation for them all. Ultimately, the child was the one who lost, and he'd be lying if he said he didn't hold a small ounce of guilt. Though he didn't completely support Cynthia's decision, he never challenged her either.

"I don't know. I really don't know. I am concerned with how Chloe and Kelly will take the news. I don't know if I should tell them now or wait to see if she chooses to contact me. I want to spare the girls the pain if at all possible."

"Cyn, I know I've never said this to you, but this is as much my problem as it is yours. I replay that time in my mind every now and then, and I shouldn't have let you walk away from her. We were partners then, and we're partners now. I should have spoken up a long time ago, but my heart was hard."

Cynthia's tears flowed freely. She didn't imagine that David would respond so kindly. But how else would he respond? Did she expect him to yell? Curse? Give her the silent treatment? She wasn't sure, but she was certain that she loved him more now than she ever did.

"Thank you honey. I can't tell you how much it means to me to hear you say that. You really are carrying some of this burden, aren't you?"

"We'll come through this all right. Don't worry about the girls. You'd be surprised at what they can handle." David intertwined his fingers in hers and lifted her hand to his lips. "I love you Cyn. Don't ever think you have to keep things from me because of your fear of how I might respond. Even if it isn't the response you want or need, please don't take my choice away from me."

Cynthia took a tissue from her purse and dabbed at his right eye. He hadn't allowed any tears to fall, but he was one moment away from watery cheeks. She smiled to herself, reminded that *the truth shall set you free*. This was the first time she'd felt free since speaking with Robert. Now if Chloe and Kelly handled the news well and she was able to work things out with her daughter when she finally met her, she'd be free indeed.

Chapter 11

Cynthia's heart raced at the sight of Chloe and Shane, Kelly and Mitchell sitting in the pews. Since Kelly married Mitchell, they only visited First Baptist Church on special occasions or when personally invited by Cynthia or David. The relief she felt moments ago when discussing her dilemma with David vanished. She needed a little more time to come up with a plan or at least rehearse her speech before telling them about the sister they had never heard of. Was this a sign from God that she should get everything out in the open today?

David gently squeezed her hand when he felt her body tense. He looked down at her and smiled reassuringly before turning his eyes back to Chloe and Kelly.

"We figured we'd surprise you all today. I hope you don't have plans, because we want to take you to lunch after service," Kelly said after standing to greet them with an embrace.

"It's so good to see you two," Chloe chimed in and followed suit with an embrace.

"Sounds good to me. I'm not passing up on a meal these days," David said with a chuckle and patted his protruding belly.

"It's so good to have you both here; of course we're going to lunch afterwards. I wouldn't have it any other way. You already know I'd be willing to make this an all-day affair. It's not every Sunday that we get a chance to do this. You're both looking beautiful today. Guys, you're both dripping swag today," Cynthia said. "Did I get that right? Isn't that what you all say these days?"

Shane chuckled a bit and said, "Close enough. Thank you, Mrs. Harrison."

Shane and Mitchell also stepped out into the aisle to hug them before sliding down to make room for them to sit on the end of the row.

Cynthia's heart was full, and for a moment her troubles dissipated. *It's going to be all right. What better time to break the news than after hearing a sermon? Maybe their hearts will be more receptive.*

When the service ended, Cynthia knew that the time to share the news was today. The pastor's sermon about fear and worry resonated with her. She'd been wearing herself out with worry and fear of the future. Besides, today's meditational Scripture reminded her that worrying didn't add a single hour to her life; it did nothing for her other than give her headaches. In the middle of the sermon, she decided she wouldn't worry about the outcome of the situation. She'd only deal with it when the time came.

"Any place you guys have in mind to eat? I'm in the mood for fish," Kelly said.

"That sounds good," David said. "Lead the way."

"I'm leaving for training in a bit, so I'll have to catch you all next time," Shane interjected. "Eat enough for me." Shane hugged Kelly and Cynthia and shook hands with David and Mitchell before walking Chloe back to her car.

"Are you going to make it without me?" Shane teased.

"Barely," Chloe went right along with him.

"Be strong CoCo. God will look after you while I'm away. These next six weeks will be behind us in no time."

"I'm counting on it; that is, for God to look after me and for you to get back quickly. I know that things between us haven't been moving as quickly as you would like, but hopefully we can get it together when you make it back to me."

"I like the sound of that. Talking like that makes me want to speed time up myself, if I'm going to have a new job and a beautiful woman by my side at the end of all this."

"You just make it back to me and the rest will work itself out."

"I'll do everything I can to make it happen." Silently he added, *I love you.* He wanted to tell her again, but didn't want the moment to become awkward or make her feel like she needed to tell him the same.

He squeezed her tightly before opening her car door. When she was inside, he kissed her cheek and walked toward his truck with a little pep in his step. He'd passed his detective exam and was excited about the training, but ready to get it over with before it even started so that he could get back to her.

The parking lot was nearly empty after she and Shane said their good-byes. She could see her sister along with her parents across the parking lot watching and waiting for her to join them.

"Ready?" Kelly asked.

Chloe nodded and waited for Kelly to input the address of the restaurant into her GPS. For the first time in a while, Chloe felt like things were really starting to come together and that she was finally ready to move out of the shadow of her marriage to Rico. She could feel it in her bones: Today was the start of something great.

Chapter 12

"Oh my goodness . . . this is so good. I think I've been eating chicken for about two months. This salmon is melting in my mouth," Chloe was the first to comment on the food, commencing the small talk they had been having before their entrées arrived.

"You all are the most important part of my life. You do know that, right?" Cynthia began, directing her attention to both Chloe and Kelly, who were sitting directly across from her and David.

Chloe and Kelly were immediately on high alert. Something had to be wrong. It wasn't like their mother to become mushy and teary-eyed for no apparent reason. Was she dying? Was their father dying?

"We know you love us, Mom. What's wrong?" Chloe asked, placing her fork on her plate and giving her full attention to Cynthia.

"Nothing is wrong, my dear. As your mother, I want you to know that I never have and never will do anything to intentionally hurt or deceive either of you."

"Okay, where is this going?" Kelly asked after taking her last bite of food. "Should we be worried?"

"Please let me finish while I have the courage to do so," Cynthia said sternly and paused. Worry was etched across her features. She now had everyone's attention. "There's a little more to the story I shared with you about me cheating on your father. You have a sister."

"Kel, honey, I'm going to take the kids to the play area," Mitchell whispered to her after Cynthia's revelation. "Unless you need me to stay with you." He figured the conversation soon to follow would not be for their children's inquisitive ears.

"No, um, yes, please take them," Kelly stammered, trying to wrap her mind around what her mother had just revealed to them. She'd always pictured her parents as having the perfect marriage, and such a revelation from Cynthia threw her for a loop.

"Wait, what's going on and why are you telling us now?" Chloe jumped in. Her mother's admission took her back to a place she worked so hard to forget—fury and betrayal. Her chest heaved up and down as she fought back her emotions.

"I'm telling you now because it seems appropriate."

"Is she here or something?" Kelly asked and jerked her head from side to side, expecting to spot someone who looked like she should be sitting at their table. But that wouldn't make sense considering she herself chose the restaurant. Working to bring her emotions in check, Kelly turned her attention back to her mother and intentionally worked to control her breathing, which was starting to escalate. She was becoming furious as she thought about every moment she defended her mother to Chloe when Cynthia first broke the news about her infidelity to their father. She had difficulty understanding what Cynthia was now saying because she was trying to piece the lies together.

Chloe, on the other hand, began laughing hysterically, shifting everyone's attention from Cynthia to her.

"You've got to be kidding me! You sat in Kelly's house putting on a show in an attempt to get me to take my lying, cheating husband back when you're the poster woman for infidelity!" Chloe continued laughing hysterically as tears began to escape from her eyes. "Tell me. To whose benefit was that? Mine? Did you accomplish your mission?"

"Watch your mouth! I'm still your mother! The point I wanted to make is that you can work through trials in your relationship if you want to make it work! So you tell me, did I accomplish my mission?"

Chloe responded by clapping emphatically, pausing each time her hands came together.

"Truth is, I don't know what to think. So many lies coming from your mouth nowadays, Mother," Chloe said curtly.

"You will not disrespect your mother in my presence," their father said firmly.

"And yet, you have no problem with her disrespecting you?" Kelly chimed in tersely. "I love you, Momma, but I don't want to hear any more of this today. I cannot believe you would withhold something like this from us for so long. What were you thinking?"

"She was thinking she wants the best for us, remember?" Chloe added. She wiped her mouth and tossed her napkin on the table along with a few bills to cover the cost of her food. She'd heard enough for today. There had to be much more Cynthia wanted to share, but Chloe wasn't ready to hear it. Her mother had done the very thing that she had a difficult time forgiving her late husband for—lied, cheated, and procreated with someone other than her spouse.

When Chloe got to her car, she hopped in, slammed the door, and sat quietly immersed in her thoughts for the moment. What was she supposed to make of her mother's admission? What was her mother hoping to accomplish with this story? Chloe wondered what part of it was a lie and if they were finally getting the entire truth this time. Was Cynthia going to look for this sister, and did she want their help? Were she and Kelly supposed to cheer and ask when this sister was coming to town for a meet and greet? Were they supposed to welcome her with open arms?

Kelly knocked on her window, peeling her away from her downward spiral of negative thoughts.

"You okay sis?"

Rolling down the window, Chloe said, "As okay as any sane person would be in this situation. You?"

"I don't know how to feel really. I mean, she paraded around my kitchen and living room telling this story about how she and Dad overcame this and that when it was really a farce. I guess she just told us what she wanted us to hear so that you would go back to Rico, and I supported her without question." Kelly paused to check Chloe's expression. She'd been running her mouth expressing her disappointment, not thinking much about what the situation might be doing to her sister. "I'm sorry for bringing that situation up again."

"No, no you're good. That's actually the same thing I was thinking. It's not your fault."

"Yea, but what are we supposed to do now?" Kelly asked and leaned against Chloe's car staring into the distance. She could see her husband and children on the playground outside of the restaurant. What was she supposed to tell them about this new auntie?

"I'm not sure. You suppose she lives here? Or in town maybe?" Chloe asked thoughtfully, still trying to figure out why Cynthia chose now to reveal this tidbit of information.

"Your guess is as good as mine honey."

"Well get back to your family and call me later. I need to go rest my mind. I'm starting to develop a headache over this foolishness."

"Same here. Love you sis," Kelly said before stepping away from the car to allow Chloe to pull out of the parking lot. She walked toward her family, who had spotted her and was walking toward her. Mitchell unlocked the car doors, turned on the air conditioner, and secured their children inside. He could see the weight on her shoulders and wrapped her securely in his arms without exchanging any words for a moment. When she pulled away, he asked, "Is everything all right?"

"It will be at some point, just not right now. Let's get home and we can talk about it later. I'm thankful for you. You know that, right?"

"Same here. I love you Kel. Everything will work out fine, I know it will."

Kelly appreciated Mitchell's confidence, and although she knew at some point things would be okay, she couldn't see past the lies and deception right now. Cynthia could have easily shared that truth with them more than a year ago. The fact that she chose to leave this sister out of the story hurt her to her core.

What other secrets had their parents been keeping for the sake of "wanting the best for them"? Would they ever be able to trust their own parents again?

∞

David squeezed Cynthia's hand reassuringly as they watched their daughters leave the restaurant in pain. David started to call them back to the table, but Cynthia stopped him, motioning him to allow them to leave and process what she'd just revealed.

"I knew it would be hard for them to hear, especially after I told them a half-truth when Chloe was going through her rough patch with Rico. But they're strong women and I know they can get through it."

"I agree. With time, they will be all right. We all will."

When the waitress arrived with the check, David slid several bills into the jacket and handed it back to her, telling her to keep the change.

"Let's go home."

Cynthia accepted David's hand as they walked out of the restaurant to be greeted by the afternoon heat. Cynthia shrugged out of her cardigan the moment she made it to the car.

"Do you think they'll ever want to meet her if she decides to reach out to me?"

"I don't know honey. I guess we'll cross that bridge when we get to it."

"Right," Cynthia said absentmindedly. She was quiet during the ride home while she gazed out the window. David made a few comments here and there, but she wouldn't be able to repeat them even if she was paid to do so. She mumbled yes and shook her head from time to time, but that was the extent of conversation from her. She was beginning to worry again about what would happen next. If her daughter were to reach out to her, she hoped that Kelly and Chloe would accept her and build a relationship with her eventually, even if they couldn't forgive her choice. Knowing that David would have accepted the child, she would have never given her up, but that was a choice that she could not change. She silently prayed that everyone involved would understand that she thought she was doing what was best at that time and that they could all work together and be a family.

Chapter 13

Two weeks had passed since Raegan and Caleb prayed about whether Raegan should reach out to her biological mother. Raegan had her phone number and address in Nashville; all she needed to do was make a move. Doing nothing wasn't working for her. The idea that there was a woman out there who birthed her weighed heavily on her thoughts no matter how much she attempted to push the thoughts to the back of her mind. She could wash, rinse, and put the dishes away and find the thought pulling at her. She could busy herself the entire day with the children, yet once they were in bed, images of Cynthia returned to her mind. If nothing else, she had to find out what the woman was thinking when she walked away from her more than thirty years ago. That was it. Closure was what she needed to continue on with her happy life.

"How are you babe?" Caleb encircled her waist from behind and planted a kiss on her neck.

Raegan folded the dish towel and stored it away, turned around in Caleb's arms, and returned the embrace.

"I'm okay, but this whole mother thing keeps bugging me. I think I need to talk to her . . . face-to-face. I need to go to Nashville. Will you come with me?"

"Actually, I have to go there for work in three weeks. Can you wait that long?" Caleb asked. That was a great opportunity to tease her about her impatience, but he remembered her persistence to get the DNA test. That didn't end well so he just left it at that.

"I can wait. That should give me enough time to reach out to her and see if she'll even want to meet with me. Besides, I need you there. I don't think I can do this by myself."

"You always have me. That is the least of your worries."

"Thanks babe," Raegan said and paused.

Stepping out of the embrace, Caleb held her at arms' length and looked into her eyes. He could sense her hesitation.

"What's the matter?"

"Do you think it's a little weird to ask my mom to come out here to keep an eye on the kids while I go seek out my birth mother?"

"Probably." Caleb chuckled softly at the thought. "But she's cool. She understands the situation you're in, right? I'm pretty sure she'd jump at any opportunity to be near her grandbabies no matter the circumstance."

"Maybe. But let's just tell her that I'm going on a business trip with you. Okay?"

"Woman, I'm not lying to your mother! You call her and tell her whatever you need to tell her and we'll fly her out. I'm not going to be party to your little scheme." He kissed her forehead and walked away. Too many lies were being told and he didn't want to be part of them in any shape or form. A lie was the reason she was traveling to Nashville in the first place.

"I love you too! You're part of this whether you like it or not!" Raegan called out to Caleb's retreating back.

"Nope!"

Raegan grabbed her cell phone from her purse and took a seat on the edge of the loveseat. She had been surprised when her father called and volunteered all of the information she was searching for about Cynthia. When he gave the phone number, Raegan took a moment and saved the information to her phone contact list. For days, she opened up the contact, but couldn't bring herself to tap the *call* icon. Glancing at the time, Raegan convinced herself that nine o'clock in the evening was too late to place a call to Cynthia and request to meet her because she was the daughter she'd given up long ago. No, she would call tomorrow for sure.

Instead, she held down the number 2 until her mother's picture and number popped up on the screen and her phone initiated the call.

"Hey Mom," Raegan greeted Marlena when the line opened. "How are you?"

"I'm doing well dear. How are you and the family?" her mother answered. Her voice seemed a bit groggy as if the ringing of the phone woke her up.

"We're all doing well. Were you asleep?"

"No, not really. I was just about to get up anyway. Looks like I missed *Wheel of Fortune* a couple hours ago," she answered when she saw the time.

"You may as well get in the bed and get your rest. But before you do, I called to ask a favor of you."

"Okay, what is it?" Marlena sat up on the couch and folded the blanket she'd been bundled in during her nap.

"I want to go to Nashville with Caleb on a work trip in three weeks. Are you willing to come out here and sit with the kids while I'm gone? I'm not sure if I will stay the entire time, but at least three days," Raegan requested and sucked in her breath while she waited for her mother to respond. Ordinarily she wouldn't be nervous about such a request, but since it was a half-truth, she was hoping her mother wouldn't be able to see through her. Marlena always had a way of knowing when she wasn't telling the whole truth, and she prayed that this wouldn't be one of those times.

"Absolutely. The blood thinners are working well to help your father manage his coronary artery disease so he's back to work, but he'll probably be jealous enough to take vacation time to come with me. You know I'm always a phone call away anytime you need me, dear."

"Thanks so much, Momma! You go ahead and get your rest and I'll wait for you to find out if Daddy wants to come before I book your plane tickets."

"I will give you a call tomorrow to let you know."

"Thanks Momma. I love you. Good night."

"I love you too. Kiss those babies for me. Good night." Marlena placed her cell phone on the charger and went to her bedroom to get ready for bed as she considered Raegan's request. She sensed a bit of hesitation in Raegan's voice and wondered what half-truth Raegan was telling this time. She wouldn't worry much because she would get to the bottom of it later. She was getting a free trip to see her grandbabies; Raegan's lies could be dealt with later.

Raegan took an audibly deep breath after she ended the call with her mother. That part was over with. Although Raegan was certain her mother knew that Cynthia lived in Nashville, she didn't question her about the trip. For that, she was grateful. The next hurdle was calling Cynthia and praying she would agree to meet with her.

Chapter 14

Cynthia's hands trembled when she picked up her ringing phone and an unknown caller with a Texas phone number glowed on the touchscreen. Though she didn't admit it to anyone, she had secretly hoped that her daughter would reach out after learning from Robert that the daughter knew of her existence.

"Hello, this is Cynthia," she answered. Her voice was a bit unsteady. She never announced herself when she answered a call from an unsaved number. The caller would be lucky if she even picked up the phone. But this time was different. She was hoping for a voice to come across the line that didn't belong to a telemarketer. A voice that should be calling her mother, but because of choices she had made, was instead a stranger seeking answers.

Clearing her throat and taking a deep breath, Raegan responded, "Hi, my name is Raegan McKinney. My father, Robert Frank Sanders, gave me your number." Raegan paused after the brief introduction. The conversation was going to be more awkward than she anticipated. She'd rehearsed a speech in the bathroom mirror about seven times before she gathered the nerve to call Cynthia, but the words seemed to escape her lips.

Cynthia didn't allow the silence to continue. It wasn't as if she didn't know who Raegan was or why she was calling. The time had come for Cynthia to revisit the past and attempt to right her wrongs in whatever way possible. She smiled and picked up where Reagan left off.

"Yes, how are you?" There were so many other things she could have said. *I'm sorry for leaving you so long ago. I hate I missed out on all of your special moments. I hope you will forgive me. I hope we can build a relationship.* But instead, she reverted to small talk. She was fumbling as well.

"I'm doing well. I'm calling because my father told me that you're my birth mother and I'd like to meet you. I'm coming to Nashville in a few weeks. Will this be okay?" Raegan's words were rushed. She held her breath in anticipation of Cynthia's response.

"Yes, of course. Please call me when you arrive and we can make arrangements."

"Thank you. I will talk to you then."

Sitting on the sofa in a daze, Raegan felt relieved and awkward after she ended the call. She did it. She called her birth mother and arranged to meet her. Cynthia's voice was calm and inviting, Raegan mused. It was as if she'd been anticipating her call. Cynthia's voice didn't hold a hint of surprise. Maybe this would work out even better than she thought, and all of her worrying about how Cynthia would receive her was in vain.

∞

"I love you Mom! Thanks so much for agreeing to keep an eye on the babies while we're away. I'll call as soon as we land," Raegan said with her arms wrapped securely around her mother's neck.

"I love you too. Be safe. The kids and I will be just fine." She waved them off and dove right in to fixing snacks for the twins and Nicholas.

"On a scale of one to ten, how guilty do you feel right now?" Caleb asked once they were safely inside their SUV heading to the airport.

"For what?" Raegan feigned innocence.

"Oh you know what I'm talking about, woman. Not telling Momma Sanders the whole truth."

"I'll tell her when I come back."

"So that means you feel zero guilt?"

"I can't give it a number right now, but I do feel pretty guilty. I just can't do anything about it at the moment. I have to get this weight off my shoulders so that things can get back to normal."

"Normal? I hate to be the one to break it to you honey, but nothing will be normal after you meet Cynthia. I think you know that already, though. Am I right?"

"Yeah, but I can deal with that, especially since I have you. I just know I can't go forward with a clear mind knowing that this woman is out there. I mean, what kind of life is she living? Do I have other sisters and brothers? What about medical history?"

Caleb nodded as she spoke, keeping his eyes locked on the road ahead while he navigated to Houston Hobby Airport. He understood the position she was in. If it were him, he would likely do the same thing. However, when he thought about Marlena he couldn't help but wonder how this would affect her. Though she knew this day would likely come, there was no way she could have emotionally prepared for it. He hoped Raegan considered the situation from all angles.

"I just want everything to work out well for all of us. Maybe I could have some kind of relationship with her at some point. Who knows? She'll never replace my mother because Mom raised me and she's all I've ever known. I'm not looking to do that. I just want to know who she is. I mean I am part of her, you know?" Raegan was speaking to convince herself more than to have a conversation with her husband. She worried about how doing this might make her mother feel, which is why she didn't tell her upfront. Hopefully she'd understand when Raegan explained it later; Raegan just needed more facts. She needed to make sense of this mess of a life.

∞

Raegan called Cynthia before she and Caleb boarded the plane in hopes of meeting her when they landed. Raegan didn't want to waste any time. If things went wrong, she could head back to Houston sooner rather than later. If things went well, she would have a few days to spend time getting to know more about Cynthia. Besides, Caleb would be in meetings most of the time starting tomorrow and she needed him by her side. Today seemed like the better option.

Cynthia requested that Raegan and Caleb meet her on the back porch of the Frothy Monkey, a local coffee shop, at two o'clock. Their plane was scheduled to arrive at twelve-thirty, so that gave them time to get their luggage, secure their rental car, and find their way to the establishment.

They arrived at the Frothy Monkey about fifteen minutes early and walked inside. The winding staircase immediately caught Raegan's eye. The shop was a bit larger than any other coffee shop she'd frequented. She assessed her surroundings, glancing at customers on their laptops and shelves lined with coffee mugs. Caleb ordered a latte for himself and a caramel iced coffee for Raegan before finding seats on the back porch.

Before sitting down, Raegan scanned the area and locked eyes with a woman seated alone at the end of the patio. Though she'd never met her, she couldn't help but feel like she'd had contact with her already. She'd aged gracefully since the time the photo was taken but Raegan knew that had to be Cynthia. Dressed in a light blue sleeveless sheath dress and white cropped cardigan, the woman stood and her lips parted into a smile. Cynthia. It had to be her.

Chapter 15

Tears erupted from Cynthia's eyes as Raegan and Caleb maneuvered around other patrons and made their way to where she was standing. Now a bit unsteady on her feet, her voice shook a little when she asked, "Raegan?"

Raegan nodded, unsure of what to do or say next. She needed to take everything in. Though she'd been trying to mentally prepare for this moment since she decided to reach out to Cynthia and again when Cynthia agreed to meet her, she wasn't ready. She thought by arriving early she and Caleb would have a few extra minutes so that she could collect her thoughts.

"May I hug you?" Cynthia asked. Her voice was uncertain and barely above a whisper.

Raegan nodded again and stepped into Cynthia's embrace. They stood at nearly the same height and Raegan could feel Cynthia's tears against her cheeks. Swept into the moment, Raegan's tears began to fall. The tinge of anger and disappointment she felt were dissipating the tighter Cynthia squeezed. In that moment, all of her questions took a backseat as she allowed herself to accept Cynthia's loving embrace and the repeated whispers of "I'm so sorry." Those words caused

Raegan's tears to flow more freely than before. Caleb remained standing behind her, gently rubbing the small of her back.

Nearly five minutes passed before Cynthia released Raegan and took a step back to assess her.

"You are so beautiful, Raegan."

"Thank you. Looks like I got it honestly. You're beautiful as well." Part of Raegan felt awkward for saying that, as if she was betraying her mother, whom she'd always credited for her beauty.

"You must be Caleb," Cynthia said after taking a deep breath and dabbing at her wet face with a napkin she took from the table.

"I am. Nice to meet you Mrs. Harrison," Caleb said as he extended his hand to shake hers.

"Please, sit down," Cynthia encouraged as she returned to the seat she occupied before the couple stepped onto the back porch.

An uncomfortable moment passed as each took a sip of their coffees and tried to figure out where to start the conversation and address the reason for the meeting.

"Umm, so thanks for agreeing to see me. I was a little hesitant about reaching out to you, but I thought it would be a good idea to meet you and hear your story."

"I understand. If I were you, I'd want answers too."

When Raegan saw that Cynthia wasn't continuing, she asked, "So why did you leave us? Leave me? Your baby."

Raegan choked back tears at the thought. She didn't think she could ever do such a thing, but then she was instantly reminded of Nicholas' mom and a hint of compassion rose within her. Did Cynthia experience post-partum depression? Did she just not want to be a mother? Was she addicted to drugs or alcohol? Or was it something about Raegan that made her walk away? Was it simply about staying with her husband? Did he not want Cynthia to keep her? Raegan's mind raced as she attempted to prepare herself for Cynthia's answer.

Cynthia folded her arms across her chest and methodically rubbed her hands up and down her arms like she was trying to warm herself, except it was about eighty-five degrees outside and warmth was the last thing she needed. However, a chill raced through her while she recalled the reason she believed she had to leave Raegan with Robert.

Would Raegan understand, or would she think she was some kind of loose woman who had no respect for her marriage? There was no telling what Kelly and Chloe thought of her right now, and she hated that she couldn't control what Raegan would think after telling her the truth.

After what seemed like hours to Raegan, Cynthia reached across the table and enclosed Raegan's hands in hers as though they were best friends sharing a heartfelt moment. Somehow Cynthia hoped that the gesture would show Raegan her sincerity and allow her to see the situation from her side.

"Raegan, darling, I've always loved you. From the moment I learned you were inside me, I loved you. There is no one anywhere that can change that." Cynthia paused and squeezed Raegan's hands a little tighter before continuing. "But at the time, I wasn't ready to raise a child. I was unfit. I made terrible choices and I didn't want to raise you in a home where there was so much stress and uncertainty. I hope you can understand that." Cynthia skirted around the truth as she tried to feel Raegan out. Her heart broke again when tears welled in Raegan's eyes and confusion masked her face.

"I don't understand."

"I was married when I conceived you, and not to your father, Robert." Cynthia held her breath as she waited for Raegan's response.

Raegan's father's recollection of the events should have prepared Raegan for what Cynthia said, but hearing it from Cynthia made the pain worse. She gently removed her hands from Cynthia's and placed them in her lap, running them up and down her thigh until Caleb caught one of them and linked his hand in hers.

"I'm sorry. I didn't want things to work out the way they did, but Robert was the best choice for you. At the time, I thought walking away from you would help save my marriage. But it wasn't until recently that I learned that was a mistake. David, my husband, didn't want me to give you up, but he never told me." Cynthia's voice was filled with regret. She hurriedly added, "Walking away from you has been my biggest regret, Raegan, my biggest regret. And if I could do it all over again, I would make a different choice. But I can't do anything about the past. I can only hope for a better future. I'd like to get to know you. And I'd like you to get to know your two sisters. Please consider it." Cynthia reached for her phone to show her pictures of Chloe and Kelly but stopped when she sensed Raegan's hesitation.

"I don't know what to say." Though hoping that Cynthia would want to begin a relationship with her, Raegan needed time to process everything Cynthia had revealed to her. In essence, Cynthia committed adultery, got pregnant, and gave her up to save her marriage. She knew she shouldn't judge, especially because of the situation she found herself in with Rico, but she found it hard to accept that her mother walked away from her. Would she have done the same thing? Raegan thought it to be unimaginable. She still had questions. Why did she cheat in the first place? At what point did she give her up? These were all minor details, and learning the answers to those questions was probably not going to make the situation better.

The defining question was whether or not she would accept Cynthia's invitation to start a relationship.

"Give me a few days to think about it. Will you? I mean, it's not that I don't want to. This is just a lot to take in. And sisters?" It had only ever been her and Eric, so part of her liked the thought of having sisters. But now a host of other thoughts flooded her mind along with a hint of excitement and anxiety. Would they accept her? Had Cynthia told them about her?

"Yes," Cynthia said, nodding simultaneously with a weak smile. "Take whatever time you need. I'll reach out in a few days."

Raegan thanked Cynthia for her time and nodded toward Caleb, indicating she was ready to leave. On their way out the door, she passed a woman standing in line who looked shockingly similar to Cynthia. And that's when she realized why Cynthia appeared to be familiar. She looked a lot like Chloe—Rico's wife.

Chapter 16

Raegan tried to ward off the eerie feeling churning away at her thoughts and stomach as she and Caleb made the short walk back to the car. Could it be pure coincidence that Chloe was in Nashville at the same time as Raegan? And not only in the same city, but the same establishment on the same day that Raegan met with her birth mother? Could Chloe be her sister? That couldn't be true, could it? Never mind the fact that Chloe's features strongly resembled Cynthia's.

Maybe she was seeing things and the lady in line only reminded her of Chloe. Though she wished that to be true, she felt something when she walked past the woman; it was the same feeling she had on the day she met Chloe in the coffee shop. She'd never met her before that day, but she recognized her the moment their eyes met. She didn't know what to call it and had no way she could explain it.

Hoping that Caleb would confirm that her eyes were playing some silly trick on her, she asked him, "Babe, did you see that woman in line who was wearing the pink shirt and blue jeans?"

"So you noticed Rico's wife, too?" He tilted his chin down slightly and gave her a sideways glance. Their eyes met briefly, but it only took one second to confirm that they shared the same thoughts.

"I wasn't sure if it was her or not. Honestly, I turned my head when I caught a glance at her and saw that she reminded me of Chloe. What is weird is that she's here and she also looks a lot like Cynthia. What do you think?" *Please tell me I'm crazy and experiencing shock,* she pleaded silently.

"What if she is your sister? Will you end your quest to get to know Cynthia and go back to Houston pretending this never happened?"

Raegan whistled as she sighed. "I don't think I'd pretend. I could just cut my losses. I mean, I've met her and she explained what happened. I've been without her all of my life, so I'm pretty sure I could go on without her. It's not like I don't have a mother." Raegan was more trying to convince herself of that option than answering Caleb's question.

Caleb used the remote to unlock the rental Jeep and helped Raegan inside before climbing into the driver's seat and starting the engine. After turning the air conditioner on, he shifted in his seat so that he was facing his wife.

"Worst case scenario, let's say that was Chloe we just saw standing in line inside of Frothy Monkey and she is in fact your sister—that doesn't mean that you can't have a relationship with her too, right? Didn't she say that all was forgiven?"

Raegan chuckled at his reasoning. "Of course that's easy to say when you believe that all is well in the world and you'll never see the mistress again. I'm pretty sure it's a lot easier to forgive when you believe all the mess is behind you. Now here I come waltzing back into her life again, and she has to be reminded that her husband cheated on her and impregnated his mistress. The icing on the cake is that the mistress is in fact her *sister*. Seeing me and knowing that I'm part of her family would probably only remind her of Rico's trifling ways."

"*Or* maybe she is stronger than you think? If you two are sisters, I'd like to believe that she's as resilient as you are."

Caleb reached for her hand and held it securely. He searched her eyes as she considered his point of view.

"You could be right, but you know you don't have to butter me up. I married you, remember?" Raegan removed her hand from his grasp and flashed her wedding band. She chuckled at her failed attempt to lighten the mood with a joke. "I'll pray about it and see how I feel led to move along. How about that?"

"You mean, we'll pray about it? Team McKinney?"

"Yes, we." That feeling of security and comfort she had whenever Caleb reminded her that she could lean on him returned, but was quickly diminished when she got the eerie feeling again.

She shrugged in an effort to brush off the feeling and buckled her seatbelt. Any seeds of doubt whether the woman was Chloe disappeared when her eyes locked with those of the woman walking in their direction. The woman nearly tripped and dropped her iced coffee on the ground when recognition set in and she recalled who Raegan was and how she knew her. Raegan wasn't the best at reading lips, but she would have bet money that was an expletive that flew from Chloe's lips at the sight of her.

"First, we can both agree that was Chloe. Secondly, I think we can agree that she wasn't happy to see me. Still think she's as resilient as I am?"

"Still doesn't mean she hasn't forgiven you."

"I'm pretty sure it doesn't mean she's ready to play nice and become family with me either."

"If it turns out she is your sister, you're gonna have to decide if you'll let your issues with her keep you from getting to know Cynthia. Cynthia has already made it clear that she wants to build a relationship with you. The guilt that you're harboring over what happened with Rico and any unforgiveness she may have has to go on the altar. Give it to God and allow Him to heal your hearts." He thought for a moment before adding, "If nothing else, you're strong. Cami, I know you well enough to know you didn't seek Cynthia, come all this way to meet her, only to allow the past to stand in your way."

"I suppose." Caleb was right. She was willing to leave the Rico fiasco behind her, but what if Chloe wasn't? Perhaps she was jumping too far ahead. She hadn't confirmed whether or not Cynthia was Chloe's mother too. There was still a possibility that Chloe just looked like her or she was related to her in some other way. Raegan had met several people in the past who reminded her of someone else and had no relation to the other. That could be the case here. Somehow Raegan doubted that though. She had to take this one step at a time and decide if she was satisfied with meeting Cynthia. Was getting to know her truly what she wanted, and was it worth risking the heartache it would potentially cause her parents and Chloe, if Cynthia was Chloe's mother?

Chapter 17

She did it. More than thirty years had passed and she finally laid eyes on her daughter again. A wave of guilt threatened to consume her all over again, but she fought hard to rise above it. Cynthia remained seated in the same position an hour after Raegan and Caleb left, nursing her cup of lukewarm coffee as she thought of the possibilities. She prayed that Raegan wanted the same thing she did. Why else would Raegan come so far to meet her? It wasn't as if they were in the same city and she only had to drive across town. No. Raegan purchased a plane ticket and flew several hundred miles to find her. That had to count for something.

What she couldn't shake was the damage getting to know Raegan could cause to her relationship with Chloe and Kelly. Cynthia had faith that they would someday warm up to the idea of having another sister and forgive Cynthia for keeping such a huge secret from them for so long. She just prayed they would get it together sooner rather than later. She really didn't want her daughters to miss out on another moment of each other's lives if they didn't have to. Though Kelly and Chloe were still upset with her, she thought it best to introduce them to Raegan while she was in town. Although Raegan said she needed time to think about it, Cynthia thought she'd try once more. Now that the lines of communication had been opened, she wanted to do all she could to keep it that way. She pulled out her phone to text Raegan. She would have liked to call, but she knew texting was what everyone seemed to be into these days. She also didn't want Raegan to feel pressured to give an answer right away, though a quick yes was what Cynthia truly desired. If she could magically make them one big happy family right now, she would do so without hesitation.

Cynthia: Hi Raegan. I really hope you'll consider meeting your sisters before you leave town. Please let me know when would be a good time for you to come over.

Cynthia read through her message several times before hitting send. It sounded important, but still gave Raegan the option to say she wouldn't have the time and maybe *next time.*

After waiting several minutes for Raegan to respond, Cynthia put her phone away, hoping she wasn't pushing her away. She pulled out a book to read and continued to sip her coffee, wanting to give herself something else to think about.

****

"What was that about?" Caleb asked. He'd glanced over in her direction several times and saw she sat gazing out the window in a daze even after they had arrived back at their hotel room.

"Cynthia is persistent. She really wants me to meet my sisters before I leave town." She shook her phone in the air with the screen open to Cynthia's text message.

Caleb sucked the air through his teeth. "So what are you gonna do?"

"I don't know, really. I mean, I did come all this way so I feel like I might as well, you know? But on the other hand, seems like we're moving a bit fast, trying to stuff years into days, if that makes sense."

"I get it. It's your call. Why don't you take a day to think and pray about it?"

"I can agree with that, but I don't want to leave her hanging and have her thinking that I'm ignoring her." Raegan responded to Cynthia's text.

Raegan: I'd like that. I will talk with Caleb about his work schedule and I'll get back to you. Is that okay?

Cynthia: It is. Thank you. I look forward to seeing you again.

Raegan left it at that.

Raegan exhaled loudly and dropped the phone in her lap. "It's done. Told her I'd get with you and let her know."

"So, was that an excuse or do you really need to get with me?"

"Well, I do need to know what your schedule is so that we can see if we have time."

"I think you know we will. You're stalling and searching for a way out, aren't you? We've come all this way. We may as well meet your sisters. At the very least, you'll be able to confirm whether or not Chloe is your sister."

"That's what I'm afraid of. I don't know if I'm ready for that. What if she is?"

"She forgave you, right?" Caleb asked again. He was there when Chloe and Rico gave their forgiveness speeches. He believed Chloe and he had an inkling that they could work past it.

"And do you remember what I told you? It's easy to say that if you believe that person is out of your life."

"Don't be so nervous. Everything will be all right. Let's give you some time to get over your jitters. Tell her we can come day after tomorrow. Is that enough time for you, nervous Nelly?"

"Ha ha. Always got a joke up your sleeve I see."

Raegan texted Cynthia her availability. Cynthia assured her that she'd work out the details and all she and Caleb needed to do was show up.

"It's done."

Cynthia's eyes lit up when Raegan responded to her text about an hour later. Her instinct was to add an *I love you* at the end of her message, but they weren't ready for that yet no matter how true it was for Cynthia. She carried Raegan around for forty weeks; there is no way she couldn't love her, though she was sure that Raegan probably believed otherwise. Cynthia couldn't blame her either. Satisfied that she'd heard from Raegan, Cynthia put away her book, pulled herself away from her seat, and made her way back to the car. She called David to give him the good news. When she secured herself inside of her car, she switched the phone to Bluetooth.

"How did it go?" he asked. His voice was hopeful. He wanted to go with her, but that was something she wanted to do alone, she told him. He obliged.

"It went well. I think she may have taken the circumstances surrounding what happened a little hard, but she seems open. I invited her over for dinner to meet Chloe and Kelly before she leaves town."

"How are you going to get them to come over?"

"I'm not. You are. I don't think they're ready to speak with me yet. Neither of them have answered or returned my calls lately. I've only gotten a dry text message here or there. Kelly hasn't even sent me any funny videos of the kids, and you know she does that at least twice a week. This has gone on for a couple of weeks now. It's about time that they put their big girl panties on and get over it. They're grown women and I've raised them better than that. And that's exactly the reason why I won't be able to get through to them, because I'd have to remind them of how I raised them and how it's time we talk about this like adults. I'm sure they won't hear that, though." Cynthia ended her ramble. She hadn't planned on rambling just now, but she needed to get it off her chest. She understood their shock, but they all needed to talk. Maybe meeting their sister would help once they saw how kind she was. They were all a lot alike.

"I'll see what I can do, but remember I'm the enemy right now as well. I kept the secret along with you."

"Yea, but you didn't sit down with them and tell them a half-truth over a year ago."

"I guess you're right about that. I'll get them over here."

"Thanks, honey. I love you. I'm going to get off the phone so I can focus on the road. I'll be home shortly."

"I love you too. See you soon my dear. Drive safely."

Cynthia pressed the button on the steering wheel to end the call. She exhaled deeply and slowly. This had to work out. Kelly and Chloe had to move past their anger when they met Raegan. She was certain they'd feel the connection and want to get to know her too . . . at least that was her prayer.

Chapter 18

"Mommy loves you all so much," Raegan cooed into the mouthpiece of her cell phone.

At least she could be at ease when it came to how things were going in Houston. Her mother was having a good time with her grandkids and they were having a blast with her. Nicholas echoed her sentiments, singing "I love you" into the phone while the twins mimicked him.

"Tell Mommy bye. It's time for milk and cookies."

"Shouldn't they be having dinner?" Raegan questioned when her mother came on the line. She wanted to fuss but she knew it would be futile against her mother.

"Who says they haven't? Besides, I'm the captain of this ship. Didn't you leave me in charge? I didn't nag you about having dinner before milk and cookies when you were little, did I?"

"Actually you did."

"Enjoy your time away with your husband. We'll see you when you get back. Say bye," her mom held the phone out so the kids could say their good-byes before she ended the call.

"Mommy is trying to boss us from hundreds of miles away. She must not know who she's talking to. I got this. Don't

I? Don't I? That's right," she continued in the baby voice that Raegan had been using moments ago.

"We'll probably have to pick up some gas drops on the way home for the kids. Momma is feeding them junk."

"Still haven't told her?" Caleb asked, disregarding Raegan's comment. His tone was much more serious.

Raegan plopped down on the hotel bed and positioned her chin on her linked fingers as she watched Caleb get dressed for the evening with the Harrisons.

"I think it's best to wait to see how things go here and discuss the details when we get back, don't you think? What good would it do to have a conversation like that over the phone? Besides, I don't want to upset her while she's enjoying the babies," Raegan counted off her reasons to keep the purpose for her trip a secret. She hoped to convince herself that she was making the right decision.

"I think we've all had a lesson in what secrets can do to a relationship," he said, glancing at her from the corner of his eyes as he tucked his black long-sleeved button-down shirt into his jeans. He grabbed his wallet, phone, and keys. "I'm ready."

Papa David managed to talk Chloe and Kelly into joining them for dinner, though he didn't tell them the entire truth. If they knew meeting the sister they recently learned they had was on the agenda, the girls would have respectfully declined the invitation, given the way they behaved when they heard about her existence at the restaurant. He, along with Cynthia, was hopeful things would be different tonight. He suggested that he'd make their favorite pasta while they talked things through as a family. He would even convince their mother to bake a German chocolate cake—a family favorite dessert. After much coaxing, they obliged, especially since they hadn't spent any time together after the ruined afternoon at the restaurant.

Mitchell stayed home with the kids while Kelly hitched a ride with Chloe to their parents' home. Kelly didn't want Mitchell involved in their family drama; she felt it was something that she needed to work through with her parents on her own, though Chloe encouraged her to include her husband.

"You sure you don't want Mitch over? I think I'd want Shane to come with me if he were in town," Chloe commented as she backed out of Kelly's driveway.

"Really? So are you and Shane on *that* level now?" Kelly eyed Chloe suspiciously; the last she'd heard, they were taking things slow. Now all of a sudden, Chloe wanted Shane involved in family matters.

"I'm only saying that he keeps me grounded and reminds me to think through stuff before making rash decisions. He's like a pillar of strength I guess."

"Pillar of strength? Whoa! I see you've got it bad, huh?" Kelly teased.

"You hear what you want to hear." Chloe changed the subject after she maneuvered onto the freeway. "You won't believe who I saw the other day, or at least who I thought I saw."

"Who, girl?" Kelly asked excitedly, turning in her seat toward Chloe and waiting for a juicy story.

"Remember Raegan? The woman Rico had an affair with?" Chloe asked, shifting her eyes to Kelly briefly to gauge her reaction.

Kelly sucked in her breath. "No way. Where?" Kelly's eyes grew wide with surprise. "What happened? Why are you just now telling me this? That's something that you should call and tell me right away!"

"So, as I was leaving the Frothy Monkey, I passed this Jeep. And you know how you can feel someone's eyes on you? I had that feeling. So I looked into the Jeep, but I didn't want to stare. I'm like 95 percent sure that it was her."

"Not that it isn't a free country, but why would she be here?"

"Really. That's a question for her. The more I think about it, the more sure I am that it was her. She looked at me as if she knew me. Then I tripped. I had to hurry up and get to my car then. That's embarrassing."

Kelly wondered whether asking Chloe about her feelings would put her on the defense. "So, how did seeing her make you feel? Like did it bring up any bad feelings? Did you get angry? Want to punch her? Want me to punch her for you?" Kelly added for laughter.

"You're too silly. I don't know. I guess it made me think about Rico," Chloe said softly.

Kelly took that as a hint to end the conversation. Some days Chloe still seemed to be a bit sensitive about his death and how things had been going prior to his passing. Given her comments earlier about Shane, it appeared she might be finally moving along and looking more toward her future.

"Time to make peace," Kelly announced when they pulled into their parents' driveway. Chloe concurred but had an unsettling feeling in the pit of her stomach.

The scent of garlic butter and shrimp greeted them when they walked inside, a smell that brought smiles to their faces and an invitation to satiate their hunger pains. Cynthia was the first to greet them with lengthy warm hugs, whispering "I love you" into their ears. She was already becoming emotional, so she fanned her eyes to keep them dry.

Engaged in small talk about the weather, work, and TV shows, they skirted around the issue at hand: the secret their parents kept from them all of their lives.

"Dinner is almost ready, but first I want to talk to you two." Cynthia led them to the living room and invited them to join her with the wave of her hand. She took a deep breath and jumped right in. No more secrets.

"Remember the sister I told you about?"

Kelly and Chloe nodded.

"Well, I met her a few days ago and she's coming over this evening. Despite my shortcomings and the mistakes I made, I really hope that you won't allow that to get in the way of you all getting to know—"

The doorbell chime interrupted her speech and they all paused as Papa David emerged through the foyer into the living room with Caleb and Raegan.

Chapter 19

"Absolutely not! Not today, devil!" Chloe all but screamed and leaped from the couch when she saw Raegan enter the room. Surely this had to be some sort of sick joke. It had to be a bad dream that no one could wake her from. Or maybe she was in someone else's dream? There was no way this could be happening to her. Now it all made sense. It was indeed Raegan she saw the other day. At least that answered Kelly's question about why Raegan was in town.

"What's wrong, sis?" Kelly asked, just as confused as their parents, evidenced by wide-eyed looks on their faces. Kelly was upset too, but Chloe seemed to be a bit rude.

"What's wrong? This is Rico's side piece! That's what's wrong. Y'all can forget it. I'm outta here! Kel, if you're riding with me, you better get your purse!" Chloe's words fired like bullets; though she only had one target, from everyone else's viewpoint, they could have all been the bull's-eye the way she carried on. She fought to control her emotions but the battle was lost the moment Raegan stepped through the door.

You forgave her, remember? Her conscience chastised her, reminding her of that day in the park when she told Raegan all was forgiven. She meant every word, at least she thought she did. She didn't have any hard feelings toward Raegan, and she had every intention of moving past Rico's infidelity with Raegan—only she didn't think the woman would be part of her life forever. This is not how any of this was supposed to work. She was to forgive Raegan and Rico. Never see Raegan again, or only in passing. Remain by Rico's side for the rest of his days. Move to Nashville and get on with her life. The mistress wasn't supposed to come strutting back into her life, reminding her of the worst times in her life, or being forever connected to her. Chloe ferociously shook her head while grabbing her purse and gesturing to Kelly to join her.

"What are you talking about?" Papa David interjected.

"This is the woman Rico slept with. Remember that whole fiasco, Dad?"

"Just wait one minute Chloe," Papa David pleaded with her. "We can all talk about this. Isn't that what we're here to do? Hash things out?" he reminded her. His voice remained calm and steady in an attempt to soothe Chloe and stop her from shouting.

Cynthia stood stone-faced at the revelation. She knew about Chloe and Rico's marital troubles, but she couldn't recall whether Chloe ever mentioned Raegan's name as the woman involved. Her first instinct was to blame herself. Had she never walked away from Raegan in the first place, this wouldn't have happened. Raegan wouldn't do that to her own sister. Or maybe if she'd only told Kelly and Chloe about Raegan sooner and they'd built a relationship long before now, Raegan and Rico would have never happened. Or just maybe if she'd never cheated on David in the first place, this very moment could have been avoided. She looked from one to the other. Raegan looked like she wanted to bolt out of the door, but was held steady with Caleb's reassuring hands on her shoulders. Chloe was ready for a showdown, arms folded across her chest, daring anyone to challenge her decision to leave.

"That's what I thought we were here to do. This just doesn't feel right and I can't stay," Chloe said.

"Wait, this is your home and I'll leave if you want me to leave. Just say it, Chloe. I didn't come here to hurt you, only to meet Cynthia's family," Raegan said in a voice so calm, she surprised herself, because inside she was a ball of knots and instinctively she wanted to do the same as Chloe—shout and leave. But Caleb made her promise to see this all the way through since she had traveled so far from home and not even told the whole truth to her mother about why she was coming.

Chloe laughed hysterically before responding to Raegan. "Are you kidding me? You're just like your mother. Why don't you stay? At least we know where she gets her promiscuous ways from." She brushed past Raegan's shoulders with Kelly on her heels, slamming the front door behind them.

Simultaneously, Caleb and Papa David held on to their wives, who were ready to pounce on Chloe. "Don't let her get to you, Cami," Caleb said to Raegan.

"That girl is so disrespectful. I did not raise her to act like that. What on earth has gotten into her?" Cynthia spoke through clenched teeth. The vein in her forehead appeared as her anger flared and tears welled in her eyes. "I'm sorry, Raegan and Caleb. Please have a seat."

Raegan hesitated, unsure whether that was the best idea. Maybe she should leave. She didn't want to cause a rift between the Harrisons, but based on what she could surmise, it was too late for that. She accepted Cynthia's invitation and slowly walked toward the sofa where Chloe had been sitting when she walked through the door.

Cynthia's tears flowed freely when she sat next to Raegan and took her hand. "This is my husband, David. And of course your sisters, Chloe and Kelly, who are probably long gone now. Allow me to apologize for their behavior. Ultimately this is all my fault to begin with. I'm sorry this evening turned out to be sour, because this is certainly not what I had in mind when I invited you over. You see, they just found out they even had another sister about a month ago when your father reached out to me. I never brought it up until now. So it isn't all you, my dear. They're upset with me because I lied to them, and I reckon Chloe is still holding on to some of what happened between you and Rico."

"I can't say I blame her. I probably would have had a similar reaction if I were in her shoes. I'm the reason her marriage fell apart," Raegan began to blame herself.

"You are not, and don't you ever tell yourself that again," Cynthia admonished. She was starting to sound like a real mother to Raegan. She softened her tone and continued. "Chloe and Rico's problems had nothing to do with you. Now you were one of the manifestations of their problems, but you didn't cause them. Besides, I know you wouldn't have given Ricky the time of day had you known he was married. I'm sure you were raised better than that."

Cynthia slipped her hands away and fanned her eyes. She thought she was over all of the emotional stuff after their first meeting, but Chloe found a way to stir her up again.

"It is great to finally meet you both. What do you do back in Houston? It is Houston, right?" David took the opportunity to chime in and give Cynthia a moment to calm her nerves.

"I'm an HR manager, but I'm only working part-time now so that I can spend more time with our children and be more involved in their lives. Working full-time and raising three children is hard. I wouldn't get to spend much time with them because by the end of the day when I would pick them up from daycare, it would be time for dinner, baths, and bed. I was overwhelmed all the time. So I guess we could say that my career is sort of on pause right now," Raegan explained.

"I see. What about you, Caleb?"

"I'm an architectural engineer. I'm actually here for a company training. So this is both a work and personal trip for us."

"Man, that's what I did before I retired. Come, let's grab a plate and I'll take you to the back and show you some of my work." Papa David was excited to finally get to share some of his work with someone who was actually interested. Cynthia would listen out of duty, but had no real interest in it. And what he did for a living was the last thing on Chloe's and Kelly's minds. All that mattered to them growing up was that he had the money to give them for new outfits or some school event.

Cynthia and David led Caleb and Raegan into the kitchen, with Raegan noticing the pictures of Kelly and Chloe on the walls as they walked by. She realized that she and Chloe resembled each other, especially as children. She wondered if that's what drew Rico to her—the striking similarities. Raegan and Cynthia settled at the kitchen table with dinner plates after Caleb accompanied David to his office.

"Can I see pictures of your children?"

"Sure!" Raegan's mood shifted to that of a proud mother when she pulled out her phone and began showing off pictures to Cynthia.

"They are all so beautiful! I hope to meet them someday," Cynthia said. Raegan allowed her full access to her phone at this point as she swiped through picture after picture, asking questions about what they were doing and where they were when the pictures were taken.

"Someday," Raegan half-heartedly promised. She wondered what her mother would think of the idea and whether or not she would be able to forge a relationship with Chloe and Kelly. Growing up with a brother was great, but it would have been nice to have a sister or two. If Chloe didn't come around, would that mean Kelly wouldn't either? Would they force Cynthia to choose? The mere thought of that seemed ridiculous to Raegan, but there was no telling what they would do, since they seemed to be a lot like her. She needed to decide for herself if this relationship was worth it.

Chapter 20

Chloe's chest heaved up and down and she banged the steering wheel with her fist while she thought about her life spiraling out of control again. She fought the urge to scream. What good would it do anyway? Though she stormed out of her parents' home like her pants were on fire and started the car, she couldn't bring herself to back out of the driveway. She was emotionally unfit to drive. Not that Kelly would have allowed her to leave in that state anyway.

"I cannot believe this is happening Kel. I mean what are the odds that woman—out of every woman in the world—is my freaking sister? Somehow this makes the whole Rico situation worse. This is crazy. Just crazy. What does Mom expect me to do? Welcome her into the family, have girl talks, get pedicures, and take shopping trips with her? Does she really expect me to share my life with that woman?" Chloe ranted. She was about to lose her mind, and the one person she could count on to be her anchor, aside from Kelly, was away in training. She'd never missed Shane so much as in this moment. A few words and a hug from him would make her feel better. He always had a way of helping her see things in a positive light.

"It's really not that bad, is it? I mean, remember you said she didn't know Rico was married. And you said that she tried to fix things. And you also said that you forgave her. So where is all of this anger coming from? Who are you really upset with here?" Kelly was upset too, but for different reasons. Their mom lied to them in the beginning and then just sprang this sister on them out of nowhere, not giving them the option of whether or not they wanted to meet her. Kelly was still working on getting over the first set of lies. She wasn't ready to meet this sister, but after seeing her, she wanted to know what she was like and hear about her childhood. Who wouldn't want to meet a long-lost sister?

"I know what I said and who I forgave, but this is different. She's a constant reminder of my failed marriage," Chloe said through sobs.

"I'm sorry this is so much harder for you." Kelly's voice was soothing, along with the quick shoulder rub.

Chloe took slow deep breaths to relax. She leaned her head against the headrest and succumbed to her thoughts while Kelly leaned against the driver's side door.

"Rico's adultery and Mom and Dad not telling us about her isn't her fault. It was those we loved and trusted who betrayed us, right?" Kelly asked thoughtfully. She was working to make sense of it all as well. She loved Chloe and would support her decision, but she didn't want her to count Raegan out for things Raegan had no control over. "We're in this together sis. Can we give her a chance? Then if we don't like her, we can cast her out like a leper!" Kelly laughed at her own silly joke. She was serious about everything she said, but she wanted to bring a smile to Chloe's face. Chloe had recently made it to a point where she was getting over Rico's deceit and death, and had decided to move forward with Shane, and then this happened. She did not need another setback; she needed to embrace love.

"You're right. I'll go back in. Can you give me a minute though? I need to call Shane."

"Sure. I'll go sit on the porch swing and wait for you before going back inside." Kelly walked the stone-lined path back to her parents' front porch and took a seat on the white porch swing. She swayed gently, not enough to alert her parents that she was outside, but enough to enjoy the cool breeze passing through. She watched Chloe and whispered a silent prayer for her. She thought Chloe was being a bit extreme, especially with the name calling, but she knew it had to be hard to learn that her ex-husband's mistress was her sister.

Chloe hooked her headset onto her ears and held down number one on the speed dial to call Shane.

"It's so good to hear your voice, Shane. How are you?" Chloe asked when Shane answered the phone. His voice alone brought peace to her heart; it calmed her unlike anything she'd ever experienced before. Maybe it was the fact she missed seeing him several times a week. Or maybe it was because he had a way of making everything seem like it would be all right.

Whatever the reason, talking to him was exactly what she needed.

Shane didn't miss the shakiness of her voice that she tried to cover up with her cheery greeting.

"Then that makes two of us. You called at the perfect time. We're done for the evening so I'm all yours for as long as you need. Tell me what's going on with you and what has you upset? I know you miss me, but there has to be something else that has your feathers ruffled." Shane added a little humor to bring a smile to her face. He succeeded. Probably anything he would have said in this moment would have done the same.

"I'm not even sure I know how to form the words," she answered with a nervous chuckle.

"Try."

The words rushed out quickly in one breath. "Remember the sister that our mother never told us about? And if that surprise wasn't bad enough, the sister is Raegan—the last woman Rico cheated on me with before he got sick." She couldn't believe she was saying the words out loud. How was any of this even possible? "And I kind of flipped out when I found out it was her about twenty minutes ago."

"Wow, I know that has to be hard on you. I wish I could be there to wrap my arms around you and make your pain go away. I'm sorry. What can I do for you from here?"

"I honestly don't know. I just needed to hear your voice and share that with you. Am I crazy for being upset about all of this? I mean, I was still trying to get over the fact that Mom lied to us all this time and hid the fact that she even existed, and then it has to be her. I thought I was over the affair and baby, but now I'm not sure that I am." Chloe continued releasing her frustration to Shane as she rested her head against the headrest, headphones plugged into her ears, and eyes closed trying to make sense of her crazy life. And to think that she returned to Nashville for a new start, only to have this happen. This had to be a nightmare that she couldn't wake herself up from.

"Before you do anything else, promise me that you'll pray about it and try to see the situation from that of your parents and Raegan. You did say that she didn't know that Rico was married, right?"

"Yea, but that doesn't really change anything that happened." Rico did this to her. Maybe she would be a bit more receptive if it wasn't Raegan or if Rico hadn't cheated with her. The one person she wished she could blame or at least shake was gone forever, so it wouldn't do her any good to harbor resentment toward him.

"I know sweetheart, but your sanity and peace of mind will depend on how you handle this. You can choose to be upset with your parents and Raegan or you can accept the facts. Now don't get me wrong, I'm not saying you have to be best buddies with her, but try to be strong. I'll be home soon to be your shoulder to lean on. I know you miss this shoulder."

Chloe chuckled at his sentiment, probably a little harder than she should have. It wasn't that funny, but there was something about the tone he used that made her crack up laughing.

"Thank you. So enough about all of the crazy stuff you're missing out on here. How is training going?"

"Very interesting actually. We've been working on our interrogation skills and surveillance techniques. That's probably the most interesting thing we've done aside from learning about case reporting and testimony. For the next couple of weeks, we'll be assigned to a specialty unit for field experience. That's what I'm looking forward to. I need a little action, because sitting here listening to someone lecture me is not really my thing."

"Sounds interesting enough. Do you know which unit you'll be with when you come back?"

"Homicide." Shane hesitated before answering. He didn't want her up in arms about his safety. With this supposedly being a bit safer for him, surely hearing the word *homicide* didn't ease her worries.

"I see."

"I can tell by the sound of your voice that you're starting to worry. I'll be fine and I'll stay safe. No way I'm going to miss my chance of cuddling up with you. You know that, right?"

"Thank you." Chloe sighed before continuing. "I'll call you later tonight. I need to go back inside and apologize to my mom and Raegan. I'm ashamed to even tell you what I said."

"No need, but let me pray with you before you go back inside. Father God, we come into Your presence to say thank You for Your goodness, mercy, love, forgiveness, and kindness. We lift up Chloe to You right now asking that You remind her of Your Word that says to cast all of our cares upon You because You care for us. Remind her that You will give her the words to speak when she doesn't know what to say. Help her remember that You are always near and You care about every detail of her life. Help her to lean and depend on You, in Jesus' name, Amen."

"Amen. Thanks Shane."

"You're welcome. I'm glad you're choosing the right thing. Besides, we all know how great you are and we all make mistakes. Try to remember that and not be so hard on yourself or them. I love you and I'll be waiting for your call this evening." The words came out of his mouth effortlessly. Though he wanted to tell her he loved her in person, he couldn't take it back now, nor did he want to.

"I love you, Shane." She finally admitted it to herself and to him, and it felt refreshing. She ended the call, prayed, and got out of the car to join Kelly on the porch.

"Look at that smile. What did Shane say to you?" Kelly teased.

"Whatever. He just does what he always does."

"And what's that?"

Make everything better, Chloe thought to herself as her smile widened, but she said to Kelly, "I think we have more pressing things to deal with." She recalled the day that she and Shane were outside playing tag the day before they started fourth grade. She must have thought she was part of someone's stunt team because she jumped over a hedge of bushes trying to catch him and skinned her knee in the process. Shane immediately ran into the house for bandages and alcohol to patch her up. He even prayed and asked God to make it better so that her first day of fourth grade would still be good. She wasn't sure why that particular thought popped into her head just now, but it was a reminder that he'd always wanted to do whatever he could to make things better for her.

"Maybe. But if Shane can put a smile on your face after that scene you put on in there, I need to talk to him too."

"Whatever. Did you call Mitch?"

"I called and updated him. He is just as shocked, but wants us to be rational about the whole thing. You know how he is . . . strait-laced. He promised to handle bedtime duty so that I can unwind in a bubble bath when I get home if needed."

"Isn't that sweet?" Chloe attempted to tease Kelly.

Kelly brushed off her comment and reached for the door knob. She rested her hand on it for a moment before twisting it open.

"Are you ready to be civilized now?"

Chloe swatted her shoulders. "You play too much, but I'm about as ready as I'll ever be. I'm counting on God to be my strength."

Taking a deep breath, Kelly exhaled and twisted the knob. "All right, here we go."

Chapter 21

Chloe's stomach tightened when she walked into the kitchen to witness her mother and Raegan laughing and talking as though they'd been doing so for years. It bothered Chloe to see them carrying on as though nothing was wrong in the world. Maybe all was well for them, but it wasn't for her.

Their mother and Raegan paused and stared at Chloe and Kelly standing in the doorway. A thick cloud of uncertainty hung in the room.

"You two can join us if you'd like," Cynthia offered and looked from Chloe and Kelly to Raegan. "We would really like it if you did."

Chloe hesitated while Kelly moved past her to take one of the seats offered to them. Kelly hoped that would move Chloe to follow suit. Chloe stood for a moment trying to think of some Scripture to support why she should be angry at her mother or Raegan, but Shane's words rang in her ear: *Try*.

Chloe walked past the table, grabbed a plate from the cabinet and prepared a plate of pasta for herself. Maybe if she could busy herself with something, that would give her time to figure out what to do or say. After piling her plate with food, she took the seat next to Kelly and sat across from Cynthia and Raegan with her arms folded across her chest. She bowed her head and prayed that God would help her to have the right attitude and to bless her food.

She couldn't stay upset forever, and sitting at the table with her arms folded across her chest made it seem as if she was preparing for war. She slowly unfolded her arms, picked up her fork, and began eating.

"Are you all right my dear?" Cynthia asked. For the past few moments the kitchen was silent as the women watched Chloe go through the motion of fixing her plate and taking her seat. Based on her behavior earlier, everyone was on guard.

"Yes. As much as I can be. I'm sorry Mom. I shouldn't have done that. Raegan, please accept my apology as well," Chloe forced the words from her lips. She was sincere in her apology, but the situation was very awkward and the only person in the room who seemed to have an issue with any of it was her.

"I understand you may need some time to process this, Chloe. I'm still processing it, but thanks. I accept your apology," Raegan said.

Kelly took control of the conversation with hopes to ease the awkward silence in the room. "Well Raegan, my issues are not necessarily with you, but with this entire situation. I mean we didn't know you existed until a few weeks ago. I'm upset with Mom and Dad for keeping you from us, but I'd like to know more about you. Are you from Houston? What do you do?"

Raegan recounted the same details she shared about herself with Papa David earlier. Her eyes lit up as she talked about her family and children. Surprisingly, Kelly found herself sharing funny stories about her own children with Raegan, picking up on where Cynthia and Raegan's conversation was when she and Chloe joined them in the kitchen. There. She had found common ground.

Chloe didn't add much to the conversation, not only because she didn't have any children, but because the entire situation felt out of place. She nodded and smiled occasionally, but mainly kept her attention on the plate and glass of water in front of her. When she finished her food, she poured herself a cup of coffee and focused on her mug more than the conversation going on around her. She may as well have not been in the room. Cynthia and Kelly attempted to include her in the conversation by bringing up memories from the years of childhood, but her inclusion only lasted for a few seconds and then she'd withdraw back into her myriad of thoughts.

"Glad to see you all came back," Papa David commented and kissed both Kelly and Chloe on the forehead when he entered the kitchen with Caleb. "Everything all right in here?" his voice boomed.

"Everything is fine. You guys done talking about blueprints and buildings?" Cynthia asked, taking their plates and placing them in the sink.

"For now."

"We need to get going," Raegan said, sliding her chair away from the table. "Thanks for having us over." Though the energy in the room was more positive than it was when she came in, she couldn't help but feel like Chloe was struggling to keep it together.

"But Caleb hasn't had a chance to try any of my cake."

Taking direction from his wife, Caleb said, "Oh it's fine. I'll take some to go if you don't mind. I have an early meeting in the morning before our flight leaves tomorrow afternoon. It's best that we get back to our room to rest up." He added a smile for assurance.

"That's fine with me," Cynthia agreed and prepared Caleb a dessert plate while the rest of the room waited in awkward silence.

"Thank you for coming by and talking work with me. I'll say a prayer for you tonight about your meeting tomorrow. I'm sure all will go well."

"Thank you, sir." Caleb shook Papa David's hand.

After handing the plate to Caleb, Cynthia wrapped her arms around Raegan and thanked her for accepting her invitation to join them although things didn't go as planned.

"Thank you all for having us. Nice meeting you, Kelly, and you as well, Chloe." The words seemed strange rolling from her lips but she meant every word. She didn't attempt to hug either of the sisters; instead she waved good-bye and shook Papa David's hand before Cynthia escorted them to the door.

"Take care of those babies," Cynthia called out to them when they reached their car.

If she never heard from Raegan again, it did her heart some good to know that she turned out all right, but she'd be lying to herself if she said it didn't matter whether Raegan wanted to forge a relationship with her. She prayed that her daughters would learn to love each other one day in spite of their past.

Chapter 22

"You handled yourself well this week," Caleb complimented Raegan as he fastened his seatbelt on the airplane. From meeting Cynthia and her family to finding out that her sister was Rico's wife, all the while providing support to Caleb during his work trip, Raegan managed to keep it all together and not lose her mind.

"Thanks, but I don't know how much credit I deserve since I wanted to punch Chloe in the face when she was shooting slugs at me. But in the midst of that I sympathized with her. I'm not sure I would have reacted much differently if I were in her shoes."

"And that's just it, my love. You didn't act on your emotions. There are a number of things you could have done or said in response to her lashing out, but you remained calm. I'm proud of you," Caleb said. He gently squeezed her hand and kissed her lips reassuringly.

After the plane was airborne and the flight attendant gave his announcements, Raegan continued, "Thanks babe. Having you by my side made a world of difference. Thank you for helping me see this through, but it's not over yet. I have to tell Mom and Dad everything. How do you think they'll take it?"

"I'm sure your dad will be okay with it but I'm not so sure about your mom. You should have been straight up with her. Something tells me she knows though. Are you ready to have this conversation with her?"

"Maybe not, but after everything I've experienced with the Harrison family over this past week, I think it's necessary." After a long pause, she said, "I don't think I'm much different from Cynthia. I mean I slept with Rico and he was married, and she slept with my dad and she was married."

Caleb shifted in his seat so that he was now facing her. "Rico is responsible for his own infidelity and so was Cynthia. You have no responsibility for the decisions they made. Don't blame yourself for that."

"Yea, but now I have to relive my mistake if I choose to take Cynthia up on her offer to keep in touch. I'll always be reminded of the mistake I made and how I helped him ruin his marriage. And that's a detail I have to share with my mom too. I don't want her thinking I'm some kind of homewrecker. Frankly I'm a little embarrassed about that."

"Cami, you're still blaming yourself. You're gonna have to choose to put that behind you. I thought you already had." Caleb adjusted himself in the seat to relax against the headrest.

"I thought so too. Out of sight, out of mind, right? But I saw the blame whenever Chloe looked at me."

Caleb stopped to accept the pretzels and ginger ale from the flight attendant. Then he turned to Raegan again and said,

"Still not your issue. She has to come to terms with the fact that Rico made a choice. You were just a participant. For her, it probably doesn't matter whether or not you knew he was married, but that's something she has to deal with, not you. Unfortunately, we can't change the past or her feelings."

"All the right answers, huh?"

"You married a wise man, sweetheart."

Raegan chuckled at his response and placed a grateful kiss on his lips. Munching on her own bag of pretzels, she mulled over Caleb's words. Everything Caleb said was right on the money, but it didn't stop how she felt. Deep down, she knew it wasn't her fault, but the look in Chloe's eyes screamed the opposite. She hurt for Chloe but she didn't know how to make it better. And surprisingly, she wanted to.

****

"We're back!" Raegan and Caleb announced as they walked across the threshold of their home. Raegan's stomach flip-flopped as the aroma of her mother's pot roast welcomed her home. Comfort food was exactly what she needed. She could only hope that a German chocolate cake or some sort of dessert would follow. Cynthia's cake had been delicious and she could use another slice or two right now.

With every step Raegan and Caleb took, the sound of pitter patter along the tile floors grew closer, accompanied by giggles.

"Mommy is so happy to see her babies. Come here!" Raegan knelt and stretched her arms wide enough to encircle Nicholas, Cassie, and Caleb Jr. in her arms, leaving Caleb to wait several moments before one of them detached from her to greet him.

"Did anyone miss Daddy?"

"Me!" they screamed in unison while grabbing hold of his legs and nearly knocking him to the floor.

"Thank you so much Momma! We really appreciate you." Raegan greeted her mother with a warm embrace, holding her tightly as if it had been years since she'd laid eyes on her and not the few days it had actually been.

"You know I'd do anything for you all. How was the trip?" Marlena stood nearly eye to eye with Raegan and studied her expression. She tucked a loose curl behind Raegan's ear as she waited for her to respond.

"It was nice," Raegan answered, glancing at Caleb and hoping that his facial expression didn't say more than it needed to. She vowed she would give her mom the whole story, but this exact moment didn't seem to be the right time. Maybe over dinner.

"Good. Time away is always good. I know you two love these babies, but spending some time focusing on your relationship is good as well. In the busyness that is life, don't forget to dote on each other," she advised, kissed their cheeks, and went to the kitchen to check on her dinner with Raegan following close behind.

"You didn't have to go all out for dinner, but I surely appreciate it. It smells so good. The aroma is making me hungry," Raegan said. She hoped her mom couldn't see through her façade. "How did you find the time to grocery shop with them anyway? It is always such a task when I do it. It takes forever to get out of the house and into the car. The time in the store becomes a chore with everyone reaching for everything on the shelves or trying to open what's already in the cart. I'm exhausted just thinking about it."

"Honey, with all of these grocery stores offering pick-up services, you still haven't tried it? You should, because it is a lifesaver. No fuss. I ordered online and went to the store to pick up. We never had to leave the car. Perfect if you ask me."

"I wasn't so sure about whether or not it was worth it, but I'll keep that in mind."

"So, what do you think about her?" Marlena asked in between checking pots on the stove and pans in the oven.

Raegan started to ask who she was referring to, but she'd always known her mother to be a perceptive woman. She no longer needed to withhold any information, since it seemed her mom knew about her meeting with Cynthia.

"She was kind and remorseful about giving me up. Part of me understands the position she was in and part of me doesn't. But there's nothing that can be done about the past. All we can do is move forward."

"So is that what you want? To move forward in some sort of relationship with this woman?" Raegan's mother spoke over her shoulder as she washed dishes, keeping her back to Raegan. Tears began to well in her eyes. For the past week, she gave herself plenty of pep talks, telling herself that it didn't bother her that Raegan didn't mention the fact that she was meeting Cynthia. She told herself that none of it mattered and that Raegan needed to do this for herself. She chastised herself for not telling Raegan sooner, but what good would that have done? Didn't she give Raegan her all? Sacrificed for her over the years and loved her unconditionally? Did that not count for anything? What did it matter that another woman birthed her? As far as she was concerned, Raegan was her child, whether or not she came from her flesh.

"Mom, are you all right?" Raegan noticed the tremble in her shoulders and went to her and wrapped her arms around her.

"Yes, I will be."

"I'm sorry if I hurt you, Momma. I didn't want to do that and that is why I didn't know how to tell you. I love you, and nothing and no one can ever change that." Raegan held her tighter as her own tears fell. The last thing she wanted to do was hurt her mom, but she wanted to get to know Cynthia too. She should have listened to Caleb and said something weeks ago. She had no idea how she could build a relationship with Cynthia without hurting her momma and Chloe. She could just walk away from the notion and get back to life as it was—except nothing was as it was before.

Chapter 23

"I, Shane McDaniels, do solemnly swear to uphold the Constitution of the United States and of the State of Tennessee. I will faithfully discharge the duties of a police officer to the best of my ability," Shane repeated the oath with his right hand raised.

There were twenty-five new officers and three new detectives at the police academy graduation and promotion ceremony at Liberty Church. Chloe's chest swelled with pride and excitement as she witnessed Shane walk across the stage to accept his certificate, embarking upon the next stage of his career. Finally something and someone else to focus on other than the mess of her life. She snapped several photos of him with her cell phone as he shook hands with the mayor and a slew of other supervisors in the Metro Nashville Police Department.

"Did you get enough pictures?" Kelly asked teasingly when she put her phone away and relaxed in her seat.

"Sure did Smarty Pants. You always have a joke somewhere, don't you?"

"I did, but now I think I'll save it for later. I have a more serious question. This man has basically changed his whole life for you by getting off the streets to become a detective. What are you willing to do for him? Is anything else holding you back?" Kelly whispered.

Chloe cocked her head to the side and shot Kelly what she hoped to be the evil eye.

"What?" Kelly asked.

"Have you been missing the past month?" Chloe's whisper matched Kelly's.

"That new sister has nothing, and I mean absolutely nothing to do with you moving on in your relationship with Shane. Don't use her as an excuse."

"I'm not using the situation, but I do think that needs to be resolved in some kind of way. Don't you agree?"

"Resolved. Yes. Interfering with your relationship with Shane? No."

There was no reasoning with Kelly, so Chloe didn't respond. She wouldn't win the argument anyway. In her mind, it made sense to have her life together before attempting to mesh her life with someone else's, causing them both unnecessary pain.

"I'll say this and then I'll leave it alone. First, if you keep on, he'll be detecting love somewhere else. Second, if you wait for perfect conditions, you'll never have another relationship. Third, don't make this decision for him. You've already made up in your mind that you need to put this thing between the two of you on hold a little longer. At least give him an opportunity to decide this with you. Don't make the decision without him."

"You have all the answers don't you?"

"Always. All you have to do is ask," Kelly said with a wink.

Nudging Kelly with her shoulder, Chloe tried to dismiss her comments. "Hush. You're interrupting the ceremony."

Kelly sat quietly through the remainder of the program, satisfied that she'd given Chloe something to think about. With the furrow in Chloe's brow, Kelly could tell that she was thinking about her advice. Hopefully she would do more than think about it, and allow it to soak in and apply it.

After the closing remarks, they maneuvered through the crowd to meet Shane in the hallway. When his eyes locked with hers, he advanced to her and lifted her off her feet as he pulled her into his arms. He hadn't seen her in days because she'd been pulling double shifts at the hospital. He kissed her briefly before lowering her back to the ground.

"Wow."

"Caught up in the moment. I miss you."

"I miss you too."

"And hi Kelly. Thanks for your support. I really appreciate it."

"Don't mention it. I'm just happy I could be around to witness this moment."

"Are you celebrating with us too?"

"Oh no. I need to get off my feet. I've been so tired lately. Besides, I know that the kids have worn Mitch out by now. I need to get home."

"Before you go, will you get a picture of us?" Shane asked and handed his phone to Kelly before she could answer.

Kelly captured a few shots, handed the phone back to Shane, hugged Chloe and Shane, and disappeared into the crowd.

Shane gave Chloe's hand a reassuring squeeze. They walked hand-in-hand through the crowd, with Shane stopping to congratulate new recruits who were in their path.

The night air was crisp and refreshing, reminding him of the new path he was embarking upon in his career and his personal life with the woman he'd loved for as long as he could remember.

"What do you feel like doing to celebrate?" Chloe asked.

"As long as I'm with you it doesn't matter. We could stop and sit right here in this parking lot for all I care. I am hungry though, so that won't work."

Chloe chuckled. She leaned against the car door and fingered the badge on his uniform with her free hand.

"I miss this. Us. Just being with you is comforting. I'm not sure I know how to explain it. It's like nothing else matters. With all the craziness going on in my life, I feel like I can handle it with you. You make things better," Chloe professed. It wasn't her intent to share her feelings right now or even that night, but the words rolled off her lips effortlessly.

"I understand it and I feel the same way. It's what I've been trying to get you to see for quite some time. I'm glad we're on the same page now. I love you, Chloe."

"I love you too, Shane. Thanks for being patient with me." There. She'd finally said it face-to-face, and she had to admit to herself that it felt good.

"You are worth the wait."

Shane pulled her into his arms and pressed his lips against hers, pouring every ounce of emotion within him into that kiss. His heart swelled with joy, knowing that he and Chloe were finally on the path that would one day lead them down the aisle into forever, hopefully.

Chapter 24

"Surprise!"

Shane's heart throbbed in his chest from the unanticipated sound of cheers and lights flickering on when he followed Chloe into her apartment. She'd told him that she wanted to change clothes before they went out for dinner.

Black and gold balloons floated around the apartment, complementing the congratulatory sign adorned with police badges that hung on the wall of Chloe's living area. The guests also wore badges with handwritten special messages for Shane.

"C'mon now. Did you really think I wasn't prepared?" Chloe asked and turned to throw her arms around his neck again. "I'm proud of you and there was no way I could let you accomplish one of your dreams and not celebrate you."

He squeezed her with excitement before releasing her and accepting hugs and congratulatory remarks from the guests, which consisted of Chloe's parents, Kelly's family, his mother and father, and a couple of his officer friends that he and Chloe knew from high school.

"You're so handsome and Momma is so proud of you, Son. You've done well. You just do everything in your power to come home every night. All I ever wanted was for you to be safe."

"Come here, Son." Shane's father hugged him and slapped him on the back a few times. "Proud of you. Sorry we had to lie to you about tonight, but we promised Chloe we'd help her out here." They'd told him that his mother's arthritis was acting up again and that they had to miss the ceremony. However, they managed to hold seats in the back of the church and skip out without being noticed so that they could make it back in enough time for the celebration.

"I'm just happy to see you two here. I love you both."

"Back to a struggling Mitch, huh?" Shane accused when he made it to Kelly.

"It was a half-truth. He was struggling in keeping the kids from destroying all of these decorations, so I needed to get here to help him out. Congrats on your promotion, dude." Kelly tapped his shoulder before pulling him into a quick hug.

"Thanks, Kelly."

"I had it all under control. Never mind Kelly. Congrats, bro."

Shane chuckled and clasped one of Mitchell's hands, pulled him close, and patted his back with the other. "Thanks, man."

"We are so proud of you. Not only are you making a difference in our city, you're making a difference in the life of our daughter, and for that, I am grateful. So proud of you Shane, so proud. Congratulations, my dear," Cynthia Harrison said and pulled Shane into an embrace. She then whispered, "She needs your strength right now. Please help her through this." She winked when she pulled away and Shane nodded in response as his mind quickly raced to figure out what she meant. Of course, this new sister business. He shot a glance to Chloe, whose nose briefly wrinkled in disgust as she appeared to be spaced out. She must have sensed his eyes on her because her scowl was quickly replaced with a half-hearted smile. *Yea, she needs comfort, all right.* He made a mental note to make sure they talked later.

"I think they've all said it, but I'll say it again. Congratulations on your promotion. You've done well and I'm sure this isn't the last promotion party we'll be having for you."

"Look at you bro, climbing the ranks. Congratulations," David said.

"Patrol won't be the same without you," Mike added.

"Nah, but I'm sure we can catch up with a donut every once in a while," Gary quipped.

"Always with the jokes, huh Gary? It means a lot to see you three here. Thanks for coming out."

"We're proud of you making major moves, man."

Shane thanked them with a hand clasp and one-arm hug and turned to see Chloe standing behind him with a police-badge-shaped cake.

"Can't have a party without cake!" she cheered.

"Nice. Your idea I bet," Shane said. His smile reached his ears.

"You know Detective McDaniels likes to do things decently and in order. We gotta eat first," David said, peering over Chloe's shoulders at the cake.

The group separated to showcase a buffet-style arrangement of foods. Fruit trays, finger sandwiches, cocktail shrimp, artichoke-and cheese-stuffed mushrooms, chicken apple salad, turkey meatballs, parmesan spinach balls, and chicken skewers adorned the black and gold tablecloth-covered table. The cake was the finishing touch.

"Wow. You all have outdone yourselves. I appreciate all this love you guys are showing me. Nice looking spread. Now I honestly don't know what some of this stuff is, but I can't wait to try it."

Shane grabbed a clear plastic dinner plate and added a little of each food. Everyone else followed suit.

"You are amazing, but you know that already, right?" Shane complimented Chloe while their guests loaded their plates with food.

"Yea, I kinda do, but I wanted you to know tonight just how amazing you are. This is huge for you."

"Not just me. Us. All of this is the start of something great for us," Shane added and gestured with the hand that held the fork. "Knowing that you all went through the trouble to do this for me means a lot. I don't even know if I have enough words to say thanks."

"Thanks is enough. We all love and care for you, so it was easy."

Shane stepped closer to her, lowered his voice so that only she could hear him, and said, "Knowing you do is all that matters."

Chloe's heart raced at Shane's closeness and sentiments. It wasn't really about what he said, it was more how he said it. The love and sincerity in his tone was enough to make her throw parties for him for no reason at all. Yep, she was right. Having Shane in her life made the world around her so much easier to deal with. With the love and confidence he exuded, there was little room in her mind to think about the lies and deceit of those closest to her.

Shane and Chloe thanked everyone for coming to his promotion party. They stood in the parking lot of the apartment complex exchanging hugs, feelings of gratitude, and good-byes. Once everyone left, Shane and Chloe stood at his truck holding hands, yet silent. Cynthia Harrison's words replayed in Shane's head like a broken record. He didn't want to end the evening discussing family issues. They'd had such a great time.

"So . . . you start detective work tomorrow?" Chloe asked, her eyes fixated on the stars that lit the night sky.

"I have to work alongside a senior detective for a while before I can lead my own cases, but I'm looking forward to doing something different."

"Good. It's amazing to see that you started this year with a goal and we're not even halfway through the year and you've done it. I'm proud of you. Your persistence is motivating."

"Thanks, but do you want to know what I'm proud of?"

"What's that?"

"Having you by my side. Apart from this, your encouragement is what inspires me. You'll probably never understand the effect you have on me, but know that I appreciate everything you have done for me."

Chloe pressed her lips against his. "You're so sweet. Thanks, Shane."

After their round of good-byes, Shane walked Chloe back to her apartment and saw her safely inside before heading back to his truck to return home. It took everything in him not to play one of those sappy love songs whose lyrics spoke to how he was feeling. He was on cloud nine if there was such a thing.

When he arrived home, he shut off his engine and sat in the car for a moment, rehashing the details of the night. If nothing else was clear, he knew that he had to make Chloe his forever.

Chapter 25

Back inside her apartment, alone with her thoughts and party decor that needed to be put away, Chloe's joy began to fade. There was no longer anyone around to occupy her attention away from what was deeply troubling her. She'd come to terms with the fact that she had a long-lost sister, but why did it have to be *her*? She was trying to get past all the hurt that Rico had caused, but Raegan would be a constant reminder.

She promised Shane that she would try and she did try the evening she was at her parents' home, but to have to try over and over again, she wasn't quite sure how she would do it. With Raegan back in Houston, things were all good. However, she didn't want to have panic attacks or lash out of character whenever the woman came around again. *But is it out of character? Out of the heart flow the issues of life.* She had a silent chat with her inner self as she washed down the table and countertops, not realizing she'd been washing over the same spot for several minutes.

Her mother, sister, and Shane had helped her with packing to-go plates, cleaning trays, filling and taking out trash bags, but she still thought her kitchen needed work. She could deal with other rooms being left unkempt overnight, but not the place where she ate her food. If there was anything she despised other than Raegan and Rico's relationship, it was waking up to a kitchen sink filled with dirty dishes, crumbs on the countertop, and trash on the kitchen floor. That ground her nerves to the end.

She opened the utility room door that was right outside of the kitchen, retrieved the broom, and started sweeping like she did every night. She went through the task as she always did. It was pretty much automated. She could do it with her eyes closed, except she didn't want to leave crumbs behind. She was worn out from the festivities of the evening, but she had to get this one last thing done. Besides, as long as she was busy, it would stall the haunting that was sure to come as it had done every night since she found out that Raegan would somehow be a part of her life forever.

Though part of her preferred that Rico had not signed over the rights to his child, for her that had meant she wouldn't have to deal with the fact that Rico cheated with Raegan, and have to see her face regularly. But now, she might have to see her at family reunions or other family functions.

Maybe she was moving too far ahead of herself? Or maybe not. Chloe could tell that Raegan wanted to see Cynthia again, and it was no secret that Cynthia wanted them all to move on and bond like the perfect family.

Exhausted, she threw away the trash collected in her dust pan and tossed the broom and dust pan back into the utility closet. She washed her face and brushed her teeth, slipped out of her clothes and into an old tank top and shorts, and crawled into bed.

Tears rolled down her cheeks as she thought about her inner turmoil. *Shouldn't this be easier? God, why do I have to go through this? I know there are people dealing with far worse things in life, but this? Her?*

Chloe sat up in bed and reached over to the nightstand to grab her Bible. She hadn't consulted God since all of this started. If she didn't know anything else to be true, she knew that He was the one with answers. There was something about being honest with herself though. She knew what she was feeling toward Raegan wasn't Christlike and she was ashamed to admit it to herself and to God, even though He knew already.

She flipped open her Bible, but had no idea what to read or meditate on. She paused for a moment and began to pray, "Lord, I need to hear from You right now. I know I shouldn't have so much resentment toward Raegan and I know this isn't how You want me to be. So help me and guide me with Your Word. I need to hear from You. I want to be better and please You in all of this, but I don't know how. I don't want to waddle in unforgiveness or cause any more pain for my mother. Show me what to do and say. Help me to trust Your plan. In Jesus' name, Amen."

Chloe sat quietly, waiting to hear something from God. She needed a prompting, a Scripture, a song—anything that would help her move from this place. She began to feel peace in her spirit. She slowly opened her Bible and thumbed through pages. She read through the topics in her Bible verse finder and stopped when she read *Attitude*. Did she have a bad attitude? She felt like she was easygoing and kept a nice, well rounded attitude, but was propelled to stop when she read the title. She then skimmed the Scriptures and corresponding topics.

Her first stop was Genesis 4:6–7. "Why are you so angry?" the Lord asked Cain. "Why is your face downcast? If you do what is right, will you not be accepted? But if you do not do what is right, sin is crouching at the door; it desires to have you, but you must rule over it."

She knew the story of Cain and Abel. "I'm not like them, Lord. How does this apply to me?" She read it again. *Well, what is the right thing to do in this situation? Accept Raegan? Be kind to her? What? If I don't, sin will control me?*

She took out her pen and pad and began to journal. She wrote several things that could be the right thing to do in this situation and the possible outcome. Then she considered how sin could further develop if she continued down the same path. Her bitterness would only lead to more anger and resentment. In her anger, she would be sure to sin against God.

She moved on to another subtopic, "Bad attitudes lead to poor decisions," and read Numbers 14:1–4. "Ouch!" After reading about the Israelites' plan to go back to Egypt, she thought about how silly that was and how fear and discomfort can lead to bad decisions. She journaled a little more. She didn't want to be in that situation.

Was it fear in her way? Pride? She went a little further and read Proverbs 29:25. "Trusting You means safety. I get it, Lord. I want to work on this part of me, and I want Your light to shine through me. This isn't going to be easy for me, but I trust that You will be with me along the way. Please be patient with me as I lean on You to work through these issues. In Jesus' name, Amen."

Chloe closed her Bible and turned off the bedside lamp before settling into bed. A wave of peace overcame her. She had a better idea of what she needed to do, and she prayed that God would give her time to work on it and put her through the test later rather than sooner.

**

Kelly was thankful the babysitter had gotten the children in bed before she and Mitch made it home. Though bedtime wasn't that much of an issue, the kids tended to want to wait up for them when they were out on a date. Mitch paid the sitter, kicked off his shoes in the coat closet, and reunited with Kelly on the couch. She positioned her back against his chest and he wrapped her arms around her while she channel surfed.

"Why don't you just speak into the remote? You're never going to find anything that way."

"Not interested in seeing anything in particular anyway."

"All right, talk. What's on your mind?" Mitch asked.

"Chloe. Something seemed off about her. I mean, she was smiling, laughing, and having a good time, but I know her well enough to know that something is bothering her. It was Shane's night, so I didn't want to bring it up."

"Is it her or you? Did you tell her you've been talking to Raegan?"

Kelly put the remote on the coffee table and turned to look at him as if he'd grown another head. "You're not seriously asking me that, are you?"

"I take it that's the wrong question?"

"Chloe would disown me if she knew I'd been talking to Raegan. She's not ready to hear that yet. She's not ready."

"You never know unless you try."

"You weren't at my parents' house when she had a hissy fit! The girl practically lost her mind. Besides, it has to be this way for now. I'm just getting to know her and I know that Chloe will come around soon. She has to. Raegan is our sister. She just needs more time," Kelly said and snuggled back into her husband's arms.

Mitch rested his chin on top of her head and thought for a moment. "Babe, you should tell her. I know you think that isn't the best option, but hear me out. First, she trusts you. And you don't want to do anything to break that trust. You see that she's having trust issues now. Second, you said something seemed off about her. You need to make sure she's okay and that she's not falling into sin."

"Sin? What do you mean?"

"Her feelings of mistrust and anger can drive her to do other stuff that isn't pleasing to God. I just read a couple of Scriptures last night that come to mind." He paused and pulled up the Bible app on his phone so that he wouldn't misquote the Scripture. "James 5:19–20, 'My brothers and sisters, if one of you should wander from the truth and someone should bring that person back, remember this: Whoever turns a sinner from the error of their way will save them from death and cover over a multitude of sins.'" He closed the app and placed the phone on the coffee table.

"I'm not trying to get slapped and cursed out too. How do you suggest I go to her?"

Mitch chuckled at her response before his tone turned serious again. "The same way you would want her to come to you."

"Oh man of wisdom! Where did you come from?"

"Just letting God use me. I'm not even sure how I ended up in the book of James last night, because I was in the book of Psalms."

"You were right where you needed to be."

Kelly knew God had to be talking to her if He chose to use her husband to deliver a message to her. Though Mitch often read his Bible, she couldn't recall a time when he actually brought up Scripture in the middle of a conversation when they weren't already discussing the Bible or what they took from the lesson at church.

She allowed his words and God's Word to marinate in her spirit. She wanted to continue learning more about Raegan, but she was afraid of what that would do to Chloe. The last thing she wanted was for Chloe to feel like she was betraying her too. She'd gone to her sister before when she thought she was wrong, but this felt different. She didn't want Chloe to feel like she was taking anyone's side; she was only doing what she thought was right. Chloe had to understand that this was much bigger than her and Rico and Raegan's past issues. No matter the outcome, Kelly vowed to love Chloe through this mess.

Chapter 26

Marlena had a date with sunrise and her morning cup of light roasted coffee flavored with French vanilla creamer. She prepared her white wooden chair on the back patio with her favorite yellow and orange polka-dotted cushion positioned behind her back as she often did. Her Bible was open to her morning meditation with her journal and pencil beside it waiting to jot down her innermost thoughts.

She sat and sipped her coffee while the rays from the sunlight slowly came into view, staring into the distance and wondering what lay ahead for her family. Robert stood in the doorway for a long moment before deciding to join her. He kissed her lips and relaxed with his own cup of coffee with sugar and no cream. They exchanged no words at first, but their hearts and minds were connected.

She smiled and wiped a stray tear from her cheek. Marlena recounted the story of Raegan and Rico, Chloe's late husband, to Robert. That made the situation more complicated. Robert sat back in his seat soaking in the details, audibly exhaling.

"Everything will work out, as crazy as that situation is. Let's not interfere unless Raegan asks. This is something that she'll have to see through on her own. You know how stubborn she is; she wouldn't stop if we asked her to anyway. I don't want you worrying about Raegan and Cynthia."

"You're right. That girl has always had a hard head," Marlena said, chuckling at the thought. This seemed to be the perfect moment to share her other concerns and so she continued, "I've been trying my best not to think much about it. You know, for years I think I overcompensated, trying to make up for the fact that I didn't birth her."

"Darling, please—"

She held up her hand to prevent him from interrupting her.

"Remember her fifth birthday party? The bounce house, snow cone machines, popcorn machines, pony rides. Or even her sweet sixteen? We spent tons of money giving her a party and then taking her to the beach to celebrate. Or when she graduated from college and we went to Mexico? Don't get me wrong. I love her and I don't have any regrets, but I think a small part of me has always tried to make up for the fact that she wasn't fully mine."

"Now you wait. Let's not forget that Eric's celebrations were just as over the top as Raegan's were. We did the same things for him, except Mexico, but that is only because he deployed."

"We did it for him, but only because we did it for her, first. You know what I mean."

"Marlena, birthing Raegan is not what makes her fully yours. All of the love and sacrifices you've given make her yours. Raegan loves you and there is nothing Cynthia can do that will change that."

"I know. I just wish it were enough. Her getting to know Cynthia changes everything. Does it not bother you that you may one day have to see her again? Maybe at Raegan's house for a holiday?"

Robert placed his mug on the table and peeled her mug from her hands, placing her hands in his. He marinated on her words for a moment before answering. Though he considered the possibility of seeing Cynthia again, he'd long gotten over her actions. That was thirty-four years ago, and he would have been insane to hold on to that hurt for so long.

"Darling. It doesn't bother me one bit. Listen, that was eons ago, and seeing the beautiful woman that Raegan has become and the lifetime I've spent with you, Cynthia has no power over our lives. If Raegan wants to see her again or even get to know her, she has that right and I won't attempt to take it from her. But you need to understand that you've been nothing short of amazing to her, and she knows that too. I'm grateful to you for that. You showed up in our lives at a moment when we needed you the most, and you have outdone yourself. You've been a true blessing to our family. We love you, honey. Don't you ever question or forget that. You hear me?"

He flipped her wrists and placed a kiss in both hands and then leaned in to kiss her lips.

"Robert, you've always known just what to say and when to say it."

"Maybe. But everything I said is true."

"I love you Robert."

"I love you back. What's the Word for today?" Robert asked, gesturing to her Bible.

"I was just sitting here thinking and enjoying the sun and this cool breeze before you came out to join me. I hadn't gotten to it yet."

She picked up her Bible to begin reading when the telephone rang inside. They were the only ones they knew who still owned a landline. Robert excused himself to answer while she began her morning devotion.

"Sanders residence," he answered.

"Hey Dad!" Raegan said. "I tried your cell phone but you didn't answer."

"You know I don't keep up with that thing too much. It's too complicated. I only need it when I'm out of the house. Is everything okay? You don't usually call so early."

"I just wanted to check on Mom. I don't think me going to see Cynthia went over so well with her, though she seems to be keeping a brave face."

Robert was standing in the kitchen holding the phone. His wife was in his line of vision and the window was cracked, so he was certain she could hear his side of the conversation. He moved into the living room out of earshot. She seemed to be content in her morning devotion, so he figured he could talk freely.

"She's fine, but next time you need to tell the entire truth. You should have told her the real reason you were going to Nashville, and it wasn't just so that you could get away with Caleb. If that didn't bother her, it surely bothered me. You have to be completely honest, Rae."

"I'm sorry Dad. I apologized to Mom already. I just didn't know how she would take it. And I didn't want to offend her. No one could ever take her place, and I didn't want her to think that was my intention."

"I know baby girl. Have you had the chance to talk with Eric yet?"

"No, he's been pretty busy. He does know we need to talk; I guess he hasn't had enough free time as of yet. But there is something else you should know."

"What's that?"

"Cynthia's daughter Chloe, we had a previous run-in over a year ago."

"Regarding her late husband, Rico?"

"How did you know?"

"Your mom told me this morning."

"Oh." She was embarrassed all over again for allowing herself to get into the situation and the fact that she was sharing it with her parents made her even more uncomfortable.

"Raegan, you're a grown woman who is accountable for her own actions. You know all about sin, repentance, and forgiveness. Have you repented and settled things with Chloe?"

"Repented, yes. As far as things with Chloe, I thought we settled it, but now I'm not so sure."

"You cannot control other people's thoughts and feelings, but you can control your own. Don't walk around here holding on to grudges, Raegan."

"I'm not, Dad."

"I've said my piece. Now, how are you? Tell me. How was your visit? What did you think of Cynthia?" Robert made himself comfortable on the couch as he prepared to hear the story.

"She was nice and warm. I thought she'd be hesitant to see me, but she seemed to be happy. She wants to meet the kids, form a relationship, that kind of thing."

"And?"

"And I don't know. Sounds good in theory, but I'm not sure how we can work that out, especially with Chloe being all up in arms. Not sure if it's the best thing to do and I don't want to hurt Mom."

"She is fine. You pray and do what God leads you to do. No matter who likes it or what the circumstances were or are, she is your family, too. And if you want to get to know Cynthia and build a relationship with her, then you should," he advised.

"Thanks, Dad." The crackling of the baby monitors in the kids' room drew her attention. "Cassie and Caleb Jr. are up now and I'm sure Nick isn't far behind. Let me tend to them. I love you. Kiss Mom for me and tell her I'll talk to her later."

"Will do. We love you too." Robert powered off the cordless phone and rested his head against the back of the sofa. He immediately bit his tongue. It was he who had just said they would stay out of it. No matter who didn't like it, including him, he knew it was the right advice. He wouldn't dare stand in the way of his daughter getting to know the woman he fell in love with to create her in the first place.

Chapter 27

"Have coffee with me this morning before our shifts start?" Shane asked when he heard the line open. Chloe's voice was the last that he'd heard before bed last night and the first voice on the phone this morning. His request was a little out of the norm, but he had been away for several weeks and he missed her. Plus, he needed to make sure that she was doing okay. He didn't know what kinds of twists and turns his day would take, but starting it with her was starting it on the right track in his opinion.

"What time is it?" Chloe mumbled, snuggling deeper into the covers. She had yet to get out of bed and get going for the day. Her eyes were half closed when she fumbled for her phone in the darkness. The only reason she reached for the phone is that the ringing startled her.

"Six a.m. Your shift starts at eight, right?" Shane's voice was much too cheery for her to believe that it was that early in the morning.

"Something like that."

"C'mon beautiful. Say yes. You know you want to. What better way to start your day than with me?"

"Okay. I will meet you at the coffee shop on the corner near my apartment in about an hour." Her lips curled into a half smile. Though she loved Shane and the sound of his voice, she could kick him for calling her so early in the morning. That was unlike him, so she figured he needed to talk. He'd always been there for her; the least she could do was be there for him.

"Atta girl. I'll be waiting."

"K." Chloe ended the call and tossed the phone onto the other side of the bed. Why did she agree to that? And why did it feel like it was three a.m. as opposed to six a.m.? She needed to get back on some sort of workout routine. Her body was paying the price big time. She blinked several times to adjust her vision to the low level of light in the room. She could use a few extra minutes in bed, but seeing Shane before work would do her some good. She wasn't sure when she would see him again, since she had to pull a double shift tomorrow to cover for another nurse who was on vacation.

She rolled out of bed, showered, dressed in her pink scrubs, and met Shane at the coffee house down the street as promised. From outside the glass panels, she could see him inside sipping a cup of coffee, patiently waiting for her to join him. The moment she opened the door, the smell of coffee beans and fresh pastries greeted her. She adored local coffee houses, which is one of the reasons she suggested this place. The homey feel and tasty foods that you could never find on the menu of one of the large chains contributed to her fondness of the place. Plus, they knew her name. She liked that.

"You spend the night here or what?" she asked when she made it to the table after speaking to the baristas behind the register. She greeted him with a peck on the cheek before taking the seat across from him.

"Early riser, especially today. I didn't sleep much from the excitement for today." He gestured toward the barista to bring her cup of coffee. "Vanilla latte."

"Thanks." Chloe inhaled the fresh aroma before bringing the cup to her lips. After she sipped, Shane reached across the table and held her free hand.

"I know it's early. Sorry for waking you. I just wanted to see you before work today. And I want to remind you that I'm here for whatever you need."

"Thanks, Shane. I appreciate that because I might be needing some of this unwavering support at some point."

"Tell me more about that. We never got a chance to talk about the new sister ordeal. How are you handling it?"

"I don't know if I'm doing as well as I can be with it, and I don't know how to explain it to anyone so that they will understand."

Shane nodded and she continued.

"So here's this woman who slept with my husband, got pregnant, lost the baby, and I forgave her. I wasn't supposed to see her again. That was supposed to be the end of it. Now here she is with her perfect little life dancing right back into mine. I never even conceived a child with Rico and here she is with three children! It's not fair and I want to scream at the top of my lungs. I'm angry, Shane. Angry at her and at my parents. And I feel really helpless but I'm trying to get over it. I had a good talk with God last night, so I'm trusting that He will help me through it."

Chloe didn't realize that tears had escaped her eyes in her frustration. Shane slid his chair around next to her and took a napkin to dab at her cheeks. "I'm sorry sweetheart. I'm here for whatever you need. It seems like a lot to take in, but we can get through this together. Can I pray with you?"

Chloe nodded and Shane enclosed her hands in his and prayed and asked God to allow His love to flow through Chloe's heart, remind her of how precious she is in His sight, and to guide her in His truth.

"Thank you. I love you for that."

"I love you, too."

"So how are you feeling Mr. Detective?"

"A few jitters, but the newness of it all gives me something to look forward to, aside from my life with you."

Part of her wanted to warn him that he may not be ready for a life with her. A life with someone who couldn't control her attitude, her emotions, and who had no peace. But simultaneously, she was reminded of the Scriptures she read last night instructing her to trust God. That was something she had to work on . . . not just trusting Him with one little or big thing, but to trust Him with everything. So instead, she said, "I'm looking forward to what the future holds for us as well."

"Nothing or no one holding us back, right?"

"Right."

Shane stood and held out his hand to help her out of her seat. Hand in hand, they walked out of the coffee shop and to her car.

"Do me, well us a favor."

"What's that?" she asked, never breaking stride.

"Think about forever with me."

"What are you saying, Shane?"

"You heard me right. We've been doing this dance for a while and I think it's time that we move forward. Think about forever with me, and if that's what you want. I love you, Chloe, and that's what I want. I need you to be certain if that's what you want with me."

She opened her mouth to speak, but he stopped her. They stopped in front of her car and Shane gently lifted her chin so that he could look her in the eyes.

"You don't have to answer right now. No pressure. I need you to know what's been on my heart, and that's part of the reason I didn't sleep well last night. I'm excited about this—" he tugged at his uniform— "but I'm even more excited about us and our future together. I just pray to God that we're on the same page." He placed a gentle kiss on her cheek and saw her safely inside of her car.

"I'll call you later, sweetheart." He bid her good-bye and walked a few steps to his truck that was parked next to her.

Wow. Talk about something to chew on! She sat behind the steering wheel somewhat surprised at Shane's request. She knew that Shane was ready for more of a commitment from her, and as much as she loved him, she wasn't quite sure if she was ready for that now that this drama had raised its head. Sure, he wasn't Rico and he likely wouldn't do the same things to her, but how could she allow herself to trust again? *Trust God.*

Chapter 28

"Hey Raegan, what are you up to?" Kelly asked. She and Raegan had been exchanging text messages for quite some time, and Kelly thought she would take the leap and move their relationship from text to talk.

"Oh, hey Kelly. I'm fine. Is everything all right?" Since they hadn't spoken on the phone before, her immediate thought was that something may be wrong with Cynthia.

"Yes. Everything and everyone is doing just fine. I know we've been chatting our fingers off, so I thought it would be nice to call for a change to check on you and the family."

"Thanks. I appreciate the call." Raegan exhaled a sigh of relief and made herself comfortable on the couch with Cassie, who had been sick for the past few days. "We're okay. Cassie is running a fever so I took off work to stay home with her today. How are you guys?"

"Did you give her a little Tylenol?"

"No. I've been trying to reduce it without giving her medicine. It comes and goes. We've been doing the cool, damp washcloths, lukewarm baths, and increased fluids."

"I can call Chloe and ask her advice. Hold on."

Kelly switched the line over without giving Raegan a chance to respond, as if having a conference call was something they did all the time.

"Hey sis, what are you up to?"

"Work."

"Well you can't be working that hard if you answered the phone."

"Whatever. What's up?"

"What can we do to make the baby's fever go down?"

"What baby?"

"Hold on a sec," Kelly said, adding Raegan to the call. "Raegan are you there?"

"Yes, I'm here."

"Baby Cassie has been running a fever and Raegan has been trying natural remedies to keep her temp down but it keeps flaring up. Any advice for her?"

Chloe would throw any object within reach at Kelly if she could for doing this to her. But she didn't mistreat children regardless of who their parents were.

"Hey Raegan. What's the temp?"

"Right now we're at 102.5."

"Are there any other symptoms like coughing or runny nose?"

"No. She's just been lying around and not playing or eating as much."

"Take her to the doctor for an exam just to be sure nothing else is wrong, especially if you can't get her temp to decrease within the next couple of hours. It could be strep or some other virus. You want to get that taken care of as soon as possible.”

“I will. Thanks.”

“You’re welcome. I have to go ladies. Have a good day. Bye.” Chloe surprised herself at how calm she was. Her pulse wasn’t even racing during or after the call. Maybe her prayers were working and God was really helping her deal with it. Perhaps it wasn’t so bad after all. “Hmph.” Chloe shrugged and tucked her phone back into her scrubs.

“Something tells me you were itching for a chance to do that, weren’t you?” Raegan asked.

“Can’t blame a sister for trying,” Kelly said and chuckled. “I like talking to you and I want us all to get along. I don’t want to be in a position where I have to choose between the sister I’ve always known and the sister I’m getting to know.”

“I understand. This is all a little crazy for me too. I don’t think my mother is too crazy about this idea either. But it would be nice to have sisters after only having a younger brother all of my life.”

“I want us to get there. To have a decent relationship with each other. Actually, I’m going to make it my mission. By the time I’m done, we’ll all be getting together for Christmas holidays and family vacations.”

Raegan was now pacing around the living room rubbing Cassie’s back as she fell asleep on her shoulders. With the phone tucked between her head and shoulders, she continued her conversation with Kelly. "I don't know about that. Even if Chloe would come around, I'm not sure about how my mom would feel about sharing her grandbabies with Cynthia. I think we all need time to work through this."

"I agree but I just want you to know it's possible. I didn't like how Chloe acted and I know she apologized for it. I want to apologize too. I think the entire situation is a bit shocking to us all. However, I'm working on being a better woman for God and my family, and I'm trying to approach this the way I think He would want me to."

"You sound like my husband."

"And I sound like mine," Kelly said, reflecting on her conversation with Mitch. "I think the one thing we have to remember is that our parents are the ones who made the mistakes; we get to reap the benefits—a bigger family."

"You're right."

"And don't worry about Chloe. She'll love you as much as she loves me."

It was Raegan's turn to chuckle at the thought of that sentiment. Thinking about how far they would have to come—from her carrying Chloe's husband's baby to being loving sisters—was laughable. However, if nothing else, she trusted God and knew that He could make even the craziest situations work out according to His purpose. *What is Your purpose in all of this, Lord?*

"It was really nice to hear from you Kelly, but I think Cassie and I will go ahead and make the trip to the doctor before everyone else makes it home."

"Same here. I'll be in touch. I'll be praying for Cassie and you. It's no fun having a sick kid. I hope she feels better soon."

"Thanks."

After ending the call, Raegan couldn't help but thank God. Only He could have a sense of humor that would allow her to go through something like this. Never in a million years did she think she would be married with twins and a toddler and finding out another woman birthed her. Even in the midst of all of that, she had a sense of calmness that she couldn't explain. She knew that everything would be all right.

Kelly knew there would be questions from Chloe later about her relationship with Raegan, and she was ready for them. In her mind, that would be the perfect opportunity to work on Chloe to help her put her issues behind her. They were adults and just as she told Raegan, they could not spend the rest of their lives blaming one another for their parents' mistakes. If anything, it was a blessing that they had one another and she planned to do whatever it took to make sure that out of the shadows of pain and lies, God's love would blossom and win over all of their hearts.

Chapter 29

She doesn't deserve your help. But God's Word says to "Love your neighbor as yourself." Chloe's thoughts warred with the Word of God that was ingrained in her heart. After checking on her last patient, she typed a few notes in the iPad, secured it in the cabinet, and made her way out of the area to the nearest elevator. When she stepped off the elevator on the first floor, she made her way to the chapel. When she neared the front, she knelt at the altar and prayed. She was determined not to be defeated by her issues with Rico, Raegan, or anyone else who had lied to her.

"Lord, You have to help me because I can't do this by myself. I want to do the right thing and love her like You would want me to, but I'm having trouble with controlling my thoughts."

She felt her phone vibrating in the pocket of her scrubs. She didn't bother to check it; instead she remained in position long after her prayer ended. She needed to feel God's presence, to know that He'd been listening to her. She was waiting for direction. After several moments passed, God reminded her of Proverbs 3:5, "Trust in the Lord with all your heart and lean not on your own understanding."

"Okay, Lord. I'm trusting you," Chloe whispered as she stood and rubbed her aching knees. Adjusting her clothes, she walked out of the chapel feeling as if once again, the weight had been lifted off her. Although she felt as though she acted appropriately when Kelly called with Raegan on the line, she knew her heart was not in the best place, and that's what she wanted to get right. All they could hear was that she sounded pleasant and helpful, but God could see what they couldn't. And she wanted her thoughts and actions to be in alignment.

She pulled out her cell phone as she walked back to the elevator and opened the text from Shane. "Lunch?" She agreed, hoping that they could finally have some time together. For the past couple of weeks, he'd either cancelled their plans or had to leave abruptly. She hadn't been expecting his new position to keep him so busy. If there wasn't a homicide he had to investigate, there were thefts, and even a money laundering case. She hardly ever got a chance to see him. She hoped that this would only last until he started working his own cases, but in the back of her mind, she knew that likely wasn't going to happen.

She spent another hour doing her rounds until Shane came to meet her in the hospital cafeteria bringing food from Arnold's Country Kitchen and crème soda milkshakes.

"This is me trying to make up for the past few dates where I had to leave you too soon," he said, pulling her favorites out of the bag and handing the milkshake to her.

"All is forgiven." She accepted the food and gave Shane a quick peck on the lips.

Shane took her hands, bowed his head, and asked God to bless their food to nourish and strengthen their bodies. Chloe agreed with "Amen" and immediately took a bite of her food.

"So, how are you? How are things around here?"

"I'm good. Things are going well. I don't have any complaints," she answered in between bites of greens.

"That's the type of answer you give the co-worker you don't really want to talk to, but this is me. How are you *really* doing?" Shane leaned in and waited for her response. He had yet to touch his food.

"Well. I'm doing better. I feel like God is really working on me with regards to the family situation. I'm experiencing a bit of tug of war and honestly I think it's because I don't want to appear weak. Does that make sense?"

"Yes. Your pride is getting in the way. That's what it is, sweetheart. But you're going to have to fight past it. You're having a tough time giving up control of the situation. You can't fight to hold on to control and trust God to do what He's going to do. Choose. If you want God to help you, let Him, and be open about *how* He chooses to do it. So many times we don't experience God working in our lives because we think it's supposed to happen a certain way. Remember that He says, "'For my thoughts are not your thoughts, neither are your ways my ways,' declares the Lord. 'As the heavens are higher than the earth, so are my ways higher than your ways and my thoughts than your thoughts.'""

"Well go ahead and preach then!" Chloe encouraged him.

"See, look at you trying to make fun of me while I'm being serious." Shane shook his head in feigned self-pity and began eating.

"No I'm not. You are absolutely right. I believe that is the answer to the prayer I prayed earlier. Thank you for being obedient and saying that. It's confirmation that God heard me and a reminder to trust Him."

"I know it's hard CoCo, but you have to choose Him daily. I believe it will get better for you. She may just become your best friend."

Chloe had a sarcastic response lined up ready to fire, but decided against it. Shane was being sincere and she wouldn't ruin the moment.

"So enough about me. How are things going with you?"

"Honestly, it's wearing me out. You know most murders happen between the hours of midnight and 4 a.m., so you know what that means for me if I'm on call. My shift starts earlier than I want it to. But what bothers me the most is being interrupted when I'm with you."

"We both have busy careers, so we'll just have to make the most of the time we have together, right?"

"There's nothing else I'd rather do," Shane agreed and pulled out his phone. "I'm not on call this weekend, so we should be able to spend some time together, right? Do you have anything planned?"

"No. I was planning to spend the weekend catching up on Netflix shows, but that can wait since you're free. I need to do something light. How about a comedy show or movie? We could go skating. I hear they're having eighties night this weekend."

"Woman you don't want to see all these muscles out there falling down on the skating rink. I'll take a comedy show for five hundred, Alex."

Chloe nearly spat out her milkshake laughing at him. "You're funny. I'll check out who'll be in town this weekend and see if we can get tickets. In the meantime," Chloe said, checking her watch, "I need to get back upstairs so that Merline can take her break."

"Go on up. I'll clean this up."

Chloe took another long sip of the milkshake and placed it in the paper bag that Shane used to bring in her food. "I love you, Shane. Thanks for everything. I'll see you this weekend. Rain or shine." She brushed her lips against his and retreated to the elevators.

Shane cleared off the table and thought back over their conversation. It felt so good to be in her presence. He was surprised himself at his regurgitation of the Scriptures. God was clearly up to something, and he was honored to be part of it. He just prayed that he could become part of it permanently.

Chapter 30

Chloe was excited to finally spend uninterrupted time with Shane. Neither one of them was scheduled to be on call for work, so she silently prayed that nothing else would stand in their way. Her thoughts were all over the place as she took her time getting ready. With no TV, radio, or phone in her hand to distract her thoughts, she was able to focus on the upcoming events of the evening.

She withdrew the whole idea of going to a comedy show moments after she'd come up with it. She loved comedy shows, but the thought of going to one made her think of the last show she attended with Rico. And that made her think of the reason she and Rico were on that date in the first place. It was their wedding anniversary, and they were trying to lighten things up so that she could get the thoughts of Rico and Raegan off her mind. Everything seemed to lead back to Raegan, and although she was working on being kinder to Raegan, she didn't want anything to remind her of Raegan tonight. Tonight was about her and Shane.

Kelly gifted her with VIP tickets to "Shakespeare in the Park." That came at the right time, considering they wanted to do something other than go to the movies or out on a dinner date. She carefully applied a little eyeshadow and tinted moisturizer to her skin and slipped into a black cold-shoulder maxi dress with pockets accompanied by her black strappy sandals.

As she was taking a final glimpse of her appearance in the mirror, her doorbell rang. Shane had arrived. She was waiting for the call to buzz him through the gate, but he piggybacked into the complex behind someone else. She'd known Shane nearly all of her life, but tonight she was nervous for some reason. She wriggled her body in an attempt to shake off the jitters, took a calming breath, and opened the door.

"Beautiful flowers for my beautiful date," Shane greeted. "And beautiful is an understatement. You're gonna have every man at the park jealous of me tonight." Shane handed the bouquet of red roses and white lilies to her and encircled his arms around her waist for a tight squeeze.

"You need to stop!"

"Have you looked in the mirror? How can I?"

"Thanks Shane the mane!" she teased and invited him inside while she placed the bouquet on the kitchen table.

"You did not go there!" Shane exclaimed, doubling over in laughter at Chloe's reference to a nickname he was dubbed in high school for his skills on the basketball court and because most of the girls thought he had it going on.

"Well, what can I say? I'm not the only one who'll be getting envious looks. You've cleaned up quite nicely this evening." Shane wore a pair of khaki shorts with an indigo polo shirt. They both could have dressed down a little more considering they were going to spend the evening outdoors.

"I didn't want to make you look bad. I knew you would go all out. I need to look worthy of being by your side, you know?"

"You're so extra."

"Extra or not, I'm being honest. You look amazing and I'm glad I get to spend this night with you. Ready?" Leaving was the opposite of what Shane was thinking. He wanted to pull her into his arms and kiss her until she couldn't breathe, but yielding to temptation wasn't on his agenda.

Chloe grabbed her purse and followed Shane out of her apartment, turning to lock the door before they walked to his truck. Shane surprised Chloe by holding her hand for the short distance. He never ceased to show his chivalrous side by opening the car door for her and making sure she was safely inside before joining her on the driver's side.

"How was the rest of your work week?" Shane initiated the conversation as he pulled out of the apartment complex parking lot and merged into traffic.

"Not bad. Everyone that I've been caring for is still alive and well, so that's a perfect week in my book."

Shane nodded but didn't respond. He could sense that she had something more to add.

"You know I love what I do, caring for people when they need it most. But that also tends to be the hardest part.

When we lose someone, that makes for a terrible week for me. Don't get me wrong. I know that we'll all die someday and that's just a part of life. But when you've been caring for someone, getting to know them and their families, there's something crippling about the fact that not everyone makes it out of the hospital alive and some of them without the hope of salvation."

Shane took hold of her hand to comfort her while keeping his left hand on the steering wheel.

"Sorry, that was not a simple answer to your simple question. How was your work week?"

"Crazy. Terrifying. So many things. You know it's one thing to be a patrol officer. You respond to the scene of a crime, write it up, and you're on to the next thing. You see some terrible things, but you don't have the time or capacity to get invested because of the volume of activity. But with being a detective, the work stays with you until you solve a case. I think the worst part of the job is when justice can't be served, like in a homicide-suicide case. It's like you don't get a chance to do your job. Though it's a tough job, the most satisfying part is the times when you are able to help families find closure. Just this past week I responded to a homicide-suicide scene and I felt like I knew the victim. Turns out, she'd come into the precinct a while back to file a report on her boyfriend because she was afraid he would kill her. It bothers me to my core that I wasn't able to help her. And I know we can't help everyone, but it still doesn't make the situation hurt any less."

"Shane I'm so sorry to hear that. Are you okay?"

"I'll be fine. But what's with this sorrow talk? How did we get here? We're supposed to be having a good time. This does not feel like a good time."

Chloe chuckled and agreed. "You're right. Hopefully, this will be good." Chloe gestured toward the park as they arrived and saw other guests securing their spots with picnic blankets.

"Did we need a blanket?"

"Nope. Kelly gave me VIP tickets. We'll have a gourmet picnic and seats at the front," Chloe said, fanning the tickets and wriggling her eyebrows.

"Really? A gourmet picnic?" Shane chuckled.

"Hey, I didn't write the language on the tickets."

"You have to admit that's an oxymoron!"

Chloe chuckled and said, "Hey, just go with it."

"I'm cool. I'll have gourmet sandwiches with you any day. Please thank Kelly for me."

"Will do."

As the parking lot started to fill, Shane was even more thankful to Chloe for the tickets that also granted them reserved parking. After shutting off the engine, he hurriedly walked around to the passenger's side to open Chloe's door and help her down out of the truck.

"Shall we?" Shane asked, extending his arm to Chloe.

"We shall." Chloe happily accepted it.

Once seated and served chicken pita pockets, roasted vegetables, chocolate cake, and lemonade, they enjoyed the live band pre-show entertainment. Being seated right in front didn't leave much room for conversation; instead their body language did the talking. Shane held her hand, caressing it every now and again along with pecks on her cheeks.

After the band exited the stage, they settled in closer and gave their attention to the play, *A Midsummer Night's Dream,* one of Shakespeare's works with which neither of them was familiar.

The play explores the magic of love and anything that had to do with love, and Chloe was on Shane's radar.

"So what did you think?" Shane asked when the play ended and other guests were packing up to leave. They remained seated.

"I liked it. Kind of makes you wonder if we really are in control when we're in love, you know? What did you think about it?"

"It was good, but what consumes my thoughts even more is that I want to do this type of thing with you for the rest of my days, Chloe. It really doesn't matter what we're doing, I just know that I want to spend my time with you."

"I want that, too."

"So is marriage back on the table for you, for us?"

"I think it's something worth talking about. I do know that I don't want to spend my days with anyone but you," Chloe answered, sealing her response with a kiss.

Chapter 31

Raegan fiddled with her watch as she paced the baggage claim area in the Houston Hobby airport waiting for Cynthia and David Harrison to arrive to celebrate Nicholas' third birthday. She knew it was risky inviting both her parents and the Harrisons out for the weekend, but she hoped to dispel any misgivings or ill feelings anyone had. She'd still have to work out her relationship with Chloe, but getting the parents together was more of a priority. She knew her mom wasn't fond of the idea of her getting to know Cynthia or Cynthia spending time with *her* grandkids, but Raegan thought it best that they all get to know each other and at least find it in their hearts to be cordial, because she hoped to build and maintain a relationship with Cynthia.

Wearing out the soles of her shoes wouldn't make them arrive in the area any sooner, so Raegan took out her phone and dialed Caleb, the one person who could calm her down.

"Hey hon, how are things at the house?" Raegan asked. As she sat down, the rhythm of her wagging foot matched her eyes as they darted around the area while she waited for the Harrisons to appear in her line of sight.

"We're good, Cami. How are you? Have they landed yet?"

"Yeah, according to the kiosk their flight landed about ten minutes ago."

"Everything is going to be fine, sweetie. I can hear the worry in your voice. Chill out a bit."

"So easy for you to say. You're not the one trying to round up folks who probably don't want to be in the same room with each other."

"But I'm married to the person who is."

"And yet you'll still be seen as the innocent and perfect husband. Everyone loves you. You can do no wrong in their eyes."

Caleb chuckled slightly at her response and said, "Don't be so hard on yourself. I'm sure this will go a lot better than you think it will. Besides, what grandparents won't act right for their grandkids?"

"Umm hmm. And what are you going to tell your parents when they realize they weren't invited?"

"The truth. You're trying to get your parents on the same page and you figured bringing them out for Nick's birthday would be a good idea. They'll understand. I'll just promise them that we'll have them for the twins' birthday. We don't have to worry about that. We'll make it up to them. This is far more important. I need my wife to be at her best and at peace, so if this is what it takes, let's get it done."

"You know just what to say, don't you?"

"Probably one of the reasons you married me," Caleb teased. With the Bluetooth in his ear, he sat on the floor in the children's playroom with one of the twins on his lap and Nicholas alongside him playing with blocks while the other twin slept in the next room.

"Maybe. I see them now. We'll be home shortly. I love you."

"I love you, too. Later."

Raegan could hear the faint sound of Nicholas' voice saying bye before ending the call.

"Hi! So glad you guys could make it!" Raegan greeted Cynthia and David Harrison with a warm hug. "How was your flight?"

"Uneventful and I'm thankful for that," David Harrison answered. "Did you leave the family behind?"

"Yes, sir. The twins were asleep when I left. They are a bit cranky if they don't finish their nap, and I didn't want to chance waking them up for the ride."

"Oh, I can't wait to meet them!" Cynthia exclaimed, clasping her hands.

"Great. Let's get your things and get out of here. Are you guys hungry?"

"Not really. I can wait to eat. I want to see these babies first!"

"Got it." Raegan did her best to hide her nervous laughter. At least she had several more hours before her parents arrived. Her dad insisted on driving to Texas, giving the excuse that he didn't want to be bound by a flight schedule. This was one time that she was grateful for his stubbornness.

Neither Cynthia nor David had been to Houston, so Raegan pointed out several landmarks on the way to her home. Minute Maid Park. Discovery Green. Lakewood Church. Houston Museum of Natural Science.

When Raegan pulled into the garage, she had a flashback to the moment when Caleb had first brought her to the house and announced he was buying it. A home filled with so much love and adoration. No one could have paid her to believe that all of this would be happening in *their* house.

Caleb greeted them at the entrance with both twins and Nicholas in tow.

"Hey! Welcome to Houston!"

"Oh hi beautiful," Cynthia greeted, reaching for Cassie. Surprisingly, Cassie accepted Cynthia's open-armed invitation.

"Great to see you again young man," David said as he shook Caleb's free hand.

"Same here. Please come in and make yourself comfortable."

"Thanks. Looks like my wife didn't need an invitation." He walked in to find Cynthia cooing at Cassie. Though she was a year and a half old, she found Cynthia's antics entertaining.

"We have water, soda, coffee, tea, and juice. Would you all like anything to drink?" Raegan offered.

"Bring little Caleb and Nicholas over to me. That's all I can ask for right now." Cynthia was on cloud nine and she fawned over her grandchildren, grateful for the opportunity to become part of their lives. "Nicholas, you're so handsome. Has anyone ever told you that?"

"Yes! Mommy tells me," he answered, giggling and hopping around the living room.

"And she's right. All of you are gorgeous! David, open the bag and get the gifts." David shook his head in disbelief but obliged, pulling out several outfits, dolls, and trucks. Nicholas became even more excited when David handed him the firetruck.

"That's exactly what Daddy needs to hear when he comes home from work every day."

"The batteries will run out soon. Just pretend you can't find anymore," David said. "I'll take you up on a soda now."

Caleb went into the kitchen with David following behind admiring the house.

"Your home is beautiful. How long have you been here?"

"A little over two years. Come on. Let me show you the media room," Caleb answered, handing him a soda from the refrigerator.

"Babe, we're heading upstairs," Caleb called to her on the way up.

"Okay, I'm never leaving this room," David said in awe of the hundred-inch projector screen. He plopped down into the recliner instructing Caleb to turn anything on. "You know this really means a lot to Cynthia, to both of us. It's not every day that you reconnect with a daughter you thought you'd never see again."

"Same here. Raegan is really praying that everyone can get along. She really wants this to work out."

"Yeah, Chloe will come around soon. She still needs a little time."

"I think Cami has come to the realization that it may take a while for Chloe to come around. Right now, I think she's way more concerned with her mom and Cynthia getting along."

"What do you mean?"

"She's hoping that this weekend will help."

"I'm afraid I don't follow."

Caleb thought for a moment and realized that Raegan didn't share the fact that her parents would be in town as well. Or if she did share it with Cynthia, Cynthia didn't tell David. He hated to be in the awkward position of being the one who had to break the news.

"Robert and Marlena are arriving later today." Caleb took a sip of his own soda and eyed David carefully to see what kind of reaction he would give.

David froze for a moment. After all of this time, was he ready to share space with the man who participated in putting them in this position in the first place? If Cynthia had never cheated on him with Robert, none of this would be happening right now. However, he couldn't dwell on that. He reminded himself that God is good and all things work together for the good of those who love God and are called according to His purpose. He couldn't pretend he knew what God's plan was in all of this, but he made a decision a long time ago to trust Him. Besides, Cynthia's transgression against him was more than thirty years ago. They moved past it; and nothing that could happen over the next several days would take him back to that dark place.

David took a sip of his own soda and then answered, "Raegan has nothing to worry about. I'm sure everything will be fine."

Chapter 32

The chime of the doorbell triggered a sinking feeling in the pit of Raegan's stomach. A big part of her knew she had nothing to be concerned about; they were all mature, Christian adults. They knew how to behave, even if they didn't all particularly care for one another. But a small part of her could see all hell breaking loose. For starters, she hadn't told her parents or the Harrisons that the others would be there, for fear that one would decide to stay home. Lies of omission.

Raegan excused herself and left Cynthia with the kids to answer the door.

"Mom! Dad! So glad you could make it!" She squeezed her dad and then her mom a little longer and little tighter. "I just love you so much!"

Her mom pulled away from her and eyed her carefully. "What did you do?"

"Nothing. I just missed you, that's all. No more men to leave at the altar, that's for sure," Raegan joked.

"Where are my grandbabies?" Marlena asked, moving past Raegan and following Robert through the foyer into the living room. Witnessing Cynthia nestled on the sofa with her grandbabies brought about a tinge of jealousy and discomfort. Though she had never met Cynthia, she had seen the picture of her and Raegan as a baby. She introduced herself, extending her hand. "I'm Marlena Sanders."

"Cynthia Harrison. Nice to meet you."

"Raegan, you should have told us that we were having company," her mom said.

"Yeah, but I figured it wouldn't matter one way or the other," Raegan answered dismissively.

"Actually, you would have mentioned it if you really thought it didn't matter. But to calm your worries, it doesn't. We love you, and that's all that matters," Cynthia said.

Marlena cringed at Cynthia's words and at the thought of Cynthia thinking that she could just pop into Raegan's life and act as if she'd been mothering her for the last thirty-four years.

"I know your intentions were pure, but next time you need to be honest. I never taught you to lie."

"You're right, Momma. I love you." Raegan kissed her cheek and asked, "Can I get you something to drink or snack on?"

"I know my way around here. I can serve myself, but thanks for asking. Where's Caleb?"

"Upstairs."

Raegan noticed that her father didn't hang around to get reacquainted with Cynthia. He said hello to her and the grandkids before he made his way upstairs to find Caleb. She wouldn't have expected anything different from him given the circumstances. Cordial was good though. She wasn't expecting them to become best friends, but she did want them to be in the same space on occasion without drama.

Robert found Caleb and David in the media room watching the sports channel. Robert greeted them, extending his hand to David and hugging Caleb. He didn't miss the way David cut his eyes at him, but he dismissed it. Even after all of this time, it was probably well deserved.

Caleb made a mental note to have a conversation with his wife later about putting him in such an awkward position. Anyone familiar with the dynamics of the situation would feel awkward in his position. The tension in the room was palpable.

"So how was the trip, Pops?" Caleb asked. He hoped he wasn't failing miserably at trying to ease the tension, or at least he hoped it wasn't obvious.

"Not bad. I'll take driving over flying any day. I hate to be confined to the flight schedules, especially since we're generally running behind anyway having to do one more thing. That's my wife's thing. Not mine. Given she's the one who is always putting us behind schedule, you'd think she would prefer to drive as well. I had to fight her and Raegan tooth and nail to drive out this go round. I don't know if I'll be so lucky to win again. She was too anxious to get back here to the grandkids."

"Raegan is the same way. If I can get away with it, I give her the wrong flight time so that we can make it on time."

"Smart, man."

"Don't tell her, because she thinks she's always the one outsmarting me. I let her think that though. Less drama, happier Momma."

"Cheers to that."

"We were just sitting here catching up on scores from last night's game. You still down with Redskins?"

"Absolutely! Have you seen our defense? We're cold this year, man!"

"We'll see about that when y'all play the Saints!" David interjected.

At that moment, Caleb felt like he could relax. Sports could bring men together and get them talking for hours, putting aside any differences they may have. The love of the game and their support for their favorite teams was all that mattered. They spent the next couple of hours talking football and then basketball.

There were times when David wanted to stop mid-conversation and ask Robert why and how he could have done what he did—nearly ruining his marriage—but the Holy Spirit reminded him that love keeps no record of wrongs. His love for his wife and his Savior kept his thoughts at bay, causing him to suppress them and push them back from where they came.

Now that Robert had been married thirty years, he didn't know what he would do if someone had done to him what he had done to David. Sure, he could and should have walked away when he found out Cynthia was married, but it was never his intent to fall in love with her. Friendly conversation and daily outings evolved into way more than either of them had bargained for. He was immature then, and he had wanted to apologize to David the moment he walked into the room, but thought better of rehashing the past.

Raegan peeped into the room and asked, "You guys all right? Can I get you anything?"

"We're good babe." David and Robert agreed and returned to their conversation. "Excuse me for a moment." Caleb followed Raegan out of the room and into Nicholas' room, closing the door behind them.

"You set me up." Caleb leaned against the door, folding his arms across his chest.

"What do you mean?" Raegan feigned innocence and turned to pick up toys and fold clothes to keep from looking him in the eyes. "Seems like you guys are having a good time to me."

"Your father seemed surprised to see David sitting on the couch in there. And David had no idea your parents were coming."

"I honestly thought it would work out better not telling them. That way, no one would back out because of the other."

"I get that, but you have to be honest, Cami. Even if they decided to back out, that would have been their choice. You can't take their choice away from them. Besides, you're selling them all short. We're adults and if nothing else, everyone in this house loves you and would do whatever it took to show you that. And if they didn't care for you, those grandbabies are enough to get them moving."

Raegan cut her eyes at him.

"I'm being real right now babe. And if nothing else, if you're going to keep anyone in the dark, it can't be me. At least I could have been more prepared. I'm up here just talking away and put my foot in my mouth."

"I'm sorry, my love. Will you forgive me?"

Caleb sighed and said, "You seem to be racking up on being sorry these days. I'll have to come up with a way you can make this all up to me."

"Really Caleb?"

"Yep." Caleb pulled her close, wrapped his arms around her, and kissed her lips. "I think I'm starting to come up with a few ways right about now."

"I bet."

"You know I love you, right?" Raegan nodded and he continued, "Don't forget that we're in this together. I got your back so you don't have anything to worry about."

"I know, my love. Thank you."

"And don't forget it." Caleb kissed her once more and stepped aside to release her back to her mom and Cynthia while he returned to his man cave.

Chapter 33

Raegan, Marlena, and Cynthia spent the morning running last-minute errands for Nicholas' birthday party. From getting helium balloons at Party City to picking up cakes and party platters, they were out of the house at least three hours. Normally, Raegan would have the children in tow while Caleb finished up something for work, but she was grateful to have the down time today.

There were moments when she thought Marlena and Cynthia would have a cat fight because her mother knew the children best and had been in their lives much longer, but Raegan managed to keep the peace. Raegan had already decided on a Mickey Mouse theme for the birthday party, but Cynthia thought it would be cute to have Batman party favors. Marlena immediately disagreed, saying that Nicholas didn't like Batman and he favored the Avengers. Though Marlena didn't say *If you knew him, you would know that*, it was certainly implied. Raegan's saving grace was the fact that she already had Mickey Mouse plates, cups, and party hats at home. It wouldn't make sense to switch the theme at the last minute. Besides, Mickey Mouse would be all over his birthday cake.

Raegan could sense that Marlena was concerned with being considered Grandma and not some other made-up name for grandmothers. Cynthia wasn't trying to take her place, only trying to find a place to fit in, but no one could tell that to Marlena.

When they arrived back at the house, Kensi and Darren were pulling up behind them. Raegan was excited to have her best friend living closer to her these days. The nearness made coming to a birthday party much easier, rather than having to be satisfied with sharing photos and videos.

Raegan left the work of carrying the items into the house and hurried to meet her best friend.

"I am so glad you could make it. You have no idea." Raegan threw her arms around Kensi and winked at Darren over her shoulder.

"I think I have somewhat of an idea. You're always up to something crazy. You actually need me around, don't you?"

"You're right. Come on in to my side of crazy," Raegan said, linking her arm into Kensi's. "It's so good to see you again, Darren. Are you taking care of my girl?"

Darren said, "I wouldn't have it any other way. It's good to see you again, too. Is Caleb inside?"

"Yeah, he is inside with my dad and Mr. Harrison. You can go on in." Raegan slowed her stride to hold Kensi outside for a moment.

"So what's really going on? You told me about the birth mom fiasco. I can't believe you invited them here along with your parents. How is your mom taking it?"

"Overall, pretty good, though I thought they were going to fight in Wal-Mart over party themes and favors for Nick," Raegan recalled the scenario.

"Well, Cynthia is kinda stepping into your mom's territory. I can see how she wouldn't be one hundred percent on board with this. They will figure out a way to work things out though, so I'm not too concerned with them. What I do want to hear about is Chloe. What in the world? And what are the chances of this happening? You have to have one of the most interesting soap opera type lives that I know!"

Raegan and Kensi found themselves walking down the street, arms still linked, continuing their conversation. Though it was ninety degrees outside, the interaction was natural for them. It was rare that Raegan had time alone with her best friend, even though they lived an hour and a half away from each other now that Kensi had moved to Pepperton.

"I still can't wrap my head around that, and would have never believed it if someone had told me. Although I think I'm past it, she's having a hard time accepting it."

"Yeah, but can you blame her? She's probably thinking that the devil and all of his minions are out to get her. Poor thing."

"Maybe."

"And you're one of the minions."

Raegan and Kensi shared a laugh.

"You're so wrong for that Kens."

"I know but I just couldn't resist. Maybe there's something about you that reminded Rico of Chloe?"

"Honey, I don't know and I don't even want to think about that disaster. But let me get you back to the house. I don't want Darren to think I kidnapped you, and I'd hate to see my mom and Cynthia in the house having some type of competition to see which Granny is the best."

"It would be sort of funny to see them arm wrestling. Winner takes all."

Chuckling, Raegan said, "You're on fire with the jokes today, aren't you?"

"Yea, I'm overdue. All jokes aside, I've been praying for you all. I know this cannot be an easy challenge for anyone involved. I mean, one day you're minding your business enjoying your family, and the next thing you know there's another woman out there who birthed you and her daughter is the wife of the man you slept with. You should write a book."

"I'll let you take care of it for me. I give you permission to use the craziness that is my life for your plot."

Raegan and Kensi walked the driveway lined with perennials and entered through the front door. Nicholas made a beeline for Raegan when he saw her walking through the foyer.

"Hey baby! Auntie Kens is here." Raegan lifted him from the floor to hug him.

"Happy birthday! Are you ready to party?" Kensi gathered him into her arms and squeezed.

"Mickey Mouse!" Nicholas screamed and threw his arms into the air, causing Kensi to release him to the floor.

"I think that's a yes."

Raegan caught wind of her mother and Cynthia taking care of the decorations. Raegan thought better of going to help and decided she would only do so if requested.

"Hey babe," Raegan said, kissing Caleb's cheek. She then leaned closer and whispered, "Is everyone behaving?"

He nodded and winked, mouthing "relax."

Raegan took Kensi upstairs to the play room to wrap presents. Raegan pulled several gifts from the closet and sprawled across the floor with wrapping paper, tape, and gifts. She happily changed the subject to discuss Kensi's adjustment to Pepperton and her wedding plans rather than worry about her family issues. Kensi announced that she and Darren decided to have a Christmas wedding in Virginia at the end of the year.

"I am so excited for you Kensi. Honey, you've been in everyone else's wedding; I'm glad I get to witness your big day."

"Other than Darren, there's no one else I want by my side. Thank you for being such a great friend, Rae."

"No problem. You know I love you girl." Raegan walked over to Kensi on her knees and hugged her neck.

Exhaling, Raegan sat back on her heels and handed Kensi another gift to wrap. "Looks like the Grannys have learned to work together. It's pretty quiet," Raegan said.

The moment the words left her lips, they heard glass breaking and a loud scream. Kensi and Raegan dropped the presents and ran downstairs to see Raegan's glass baking dish, filled with rotel dip for the party, shattered into pieces on the kitchen floor with Cynthia standing over the mess.

Chapter 34

"You have done nothing but make me feel unwelcomed since you got here!" Cynthia yelled, allowing her frustration with Marlena to get the best of her. Though the crashing pan startled the men and children, she had everyone's attention now. She'd tried her best to ignore the sly remarks and criticism, but she had had enough. This woman was not going to remind her at every turn of a mistake she made decades ago.

"I don't know what you're talking about," Marlena said, leaning against the island with her arms folded across her chest.

"What is going on?" Raegan asked, rushing into the kitchen with Kensi close behind. Mess was on the floor and in the air. Everyone else was silent while their eyes were glued to the women.

"She is what's going on. For the record, I'm not trying to take your place or erase any memories you've created with Raegan and her family."

"I never said that," Marlena said calmly.

"You don't have to say those words; it comes across in everything else you say and do. 'Oh, Nick doesn't like Batman. Oh, Nick likes to play soccer, not basketball. Raegan likes to dress the children this way. The twins like to play this and not that.' It's everything! Are you trying to prove that you've been around her all of her life? We get it! I get it! You don't have to broadcast it. Yes, I had an affair and yes, I missed out on every special moment in her life because Robert raised her! We all know that. You don't have to rub my face in it!" Cynthia fumed and stormed out of the kitchen, making her way through the French doors that led to the backyard patio. The heat emanating from her body was far steamier than the Houston heat. Being outside would help her cool down.

David followed Cynthia outside and worked to calm her. He massaged her shoulders and encouraged her to sit down, whispering prayers.

Raegan turned to Caleb, silently pleading with him for help. If she defended Cynthia, that would make her mom upset. But she knew Cynthia was right. She had noticed the competitive behavior in the store and wished she had done something then to stop it.

Caleb asked Kensi and Darren to keep an eye on the children while they ushered Marlena into the study to talk.

"What happened in there?" Robert was the first to jump in with questions.

"Nothing. I was only giving her suggestions on what the kids would like for the snack table when she dropped the cheese-dip dish and flew off the handle."

"Mom, the problem is that you've been doing that sort of thing all day."

"No, the problem is that you've been going behind my back with seeing this woman and inviting her to our family events. You should have told us she would be here."

"Your mother is right, Raegan, but that still doesn't give any of us the right to judge her," Robert said. "We all love you, Marlena, and no one can change that. What we all need to remember is that those children out there are watching us and soaking up our words and actions like sponges. They are learning from us, and the best way to teach them how to love others is to show them. They may not understand right now, but they will soon enough."

"Pops is right. I know this isn't the most ideal situation, and it probably could have been handled better, but we're here now. What we do now is what will count," Caleb added.

"Oh, the man of wisdom," Raegan teased and linked her hand into his.

"So, can we do this, Mom?"

She nodded.

"I don't always do things the right way, but my heart is in the right place. I love you, Mom. You've always been there for me and I'm forever grateful for that. But this is something that I think I need to do for me. Cynthia gave up her rights to be Mom, and I'm thankful for that, too, because if she didn't, I wouldn't have you."

"I love you, baby."

Raegan stepped away from Caleb and into her mother's arms and squeezed her tightly, not releasing her until her mom did so first.

"Let me go apologize." Marlena left them standing in the office while she went out on the back patio to find Cynthia.

David Harrison looked from one to the other, waiting for Cynthia's indication that it was okay for him to leave them alone. When she nodded, he squeezed her shoulder, nodded at Marlena, and re-entered the house.

Marlena pulled a patio chair close to Cynthia and took a seat. She waited a few moments until Cynthia made eye contact with her.

"I've been rude to you and that's not who I usually am nor have I taught Raegan to be this way. I apologize for making you feel unwelcomed and for everything that I've done to make you feel uncomfortable."

"I get it."

"No, I don't think you do. From the moment I adopted Raegan, I never considered she would find out about you and go looking for you one day. When I first learned she came to see you, it ripped my core because it felt like I wasn't enough, that everything that I'd ever done for her wasn't enough, because she still wanted to find you and get to know you. To me, that was ludicrous, though I never shared that with her. And to see you sitting in her living room when I arrived broke my heart a bit."

"I don't think I quite considered how you must feel."

"I don't think I've done the same for you or Raegan. So please forgive me," Marlena apologized. That felt like the hardest thing in the world for her to do in that moment, but she felt it necessary to keep a clear conscience, an ungrudging heart, and to keep the love flowing. She didn't want to be the reason that Nick's birthday party was ruined.

"I forgive you. I'm probably the worst person of all in this whole mess, and if God and David can forgive me, I can surely forgive you. We can work together for the sake of the family, right?"

"Right," Marlena agreed, extending a hand to Cynthia to solidify their agreement. "Can we go back inside and party now?"

Chapter 35

Exhausted, Raegan and Caleb sprawled across the sofa while their children napped. Raegan thought she'd never be happy to see the weekend end, but this was definitely one time she was glad to welcome the weekdays, grateful that Caleb was home with her today.

Having both her parents along with Cynthia and David over for Nick's party was more than she bargained for, but she was thankful that her parents were able to work things out and behave out of their love for her and the family.

"Remind me not to pull anything like that again," Raegan said, nudging Caleb's shoulders.

"Are you going to listen if I do?"

"Maybe. Today's me would like to say yes, but you know how I am when it comes to wanting to surprise people and sometimes wearing rose-colored glasses."

"Yeah, I do, but that's one of the many reasons I love you—because you see the glass half full and you believe that things will always turn out well. I'm just thankful that this time it did. I was worried a few times throughout the weekend."

"You?! No, me. I thought World War Three was about to start in that kitchen when Cynthia dropped that dish. Oh man my stomach sunk so far down. I thought I was going to lose it."

Caleb chuckled and said, "But you handled it all with grace. You were very calm, and that is why I think none of the kids worried about it too much. They always look to you to see how you will respond. Have you noticed that?"

"I guess I hadn't thought about that."

"It's true. When you walked in, their little eyes were glued on you. If you had lost control, their meltdowns would have been right behind yours, and then it would have been an even bigger mess. But my baby was a queen," Caleb complimented her and leaned over to kiss her forehead.

"Thanks babe. Having you in my corner made all the difference. You handled the situation well. All of it. Especially finding out that I didn't communicate to them who would all be here. Now *that* I won't do again. Promise."

"That's all I ask. We're Team McKinney. Don't forget that."

∞

Later that evening, Raegan's computer lit up from the Skype call coming through from Eric. She leaped toward the machine, not daring to miss his call. She'd been trying to get in contact with him for a few weeks now.

"Hey sis! Sorry I haven't been able to get back with you before now. How's the fam?" Eric asked.

"Dude! I've been blowing you up!" Raegan was relieved to finally hear from her brother. For one, seeing his face gave her peace that he was all right. She also needed to talk to him. Although Caleb had been her rock through this whole ordeal, for some reason, she needed reassurance from Eric as well.

Eric's face twisted in a scowl on the computer screen.

"Sorry. Bad choice of words given your current situation." One glimpse at Eric's uniform reminded Raegan that was probably the last phrase that he wanted to hear. Words spoken lightly had quite a literal meaning for him.

"Exactly. What's going on?"

"Caleb and the babies are fine, but I don't know what to say about myself." She leaned forward with her elbows on the desk, inhaled deeply, and stared into her brother's eyes through the screen.

"What's the matter big sis?"

"Technically, I'm your half-sister. Turns out Marlena is not my biological mom."

In just as much disbelief as Raegan was in the moment she found out the truth, Eric sat there, stunned and speechless.

"Say something."

"I don't understand. Explain to me what's going on around there."

Raegan did her best to summarize the circumstances in the limited amount of time she knew they had, filling in as many blanks as she could so that Eric would have the complete picture.

"Well, I don't care who your momma is or isn't. That doesn't change anything between us, okay? I can't say I know exactly how you feel, but I have an idea. Is Caleb holding you down?"

"Yeah, he's being Caleb. Strong and loving. I'm glad he's here."

"I'm glad you've got him too. I know I missed a lot of what's happening around there, but you know I love you, sis, and you can depend on me for support. And no matter what, you know God's got you, right?"

"Right."

"You're strong and I've always admired your faith. Don't forget that Scripture that you always quote."

"And what Scripture is that?"

"All things work together for the good of those who love God and are called according to His purpose."

"Amen."

"No stressing, okay?"

Raegan nodded, placed a kiss on her index and middle finger and pressed them to the screen. "I love you, dude. How are you? Who's taking care of you out there?"

Eric chuckled before answering, "I'm chill right now. I'm handling myself."

"Umm hmm. I'm just saying that I would feel better knowing that someone had your back out there."

"I have an entire battalion who has my back."

"You know exactly what I mean."

"Yeah, I do. You'll be the first to know when there is someone special. Alright? Gotta go. I'll check on you soon. Love you, sis."

"Love you, too." Raegan repeated the motion of placing a kiss on the screen. She closed the lid to her laptop, repeating the Scripture. She smiled at the thought of God using the conversation with Eric to remind her that He is always with her. The mere thought of Eric even remembering any Scripture made her heart swell with joy and comfort. God was watching over him, too.

∞

Shane and Chloe settled into their seats at the end of praise and worship to prepare to hear Pastor Jacob's message, "I Dare You to Dream Again." Before Chloe had heard a word from the sermon, something stirred within her. From the moment she learned of Rico's affair with Raegan, her life had spiraled out of control and her dreams and desires had been locked away. Dreams that she forgot she even had. Desires that were stolen from her heart and thoughts when she had to deal with his transgressions, his sickness, and ultimately his death.

"Dreams are released through prayer and the Word. See, look at Habakkuk 2:1. He was in his watchtower, which tells us that he had to get away from the noise and busyness of everyday life. Church, if you're gonna get God dreams, you have to draw away daily, withdraw weekly, and abandon annually. I still can't get an amen. Look at Proverbs 29:18. We perish for lack of vision, church! And to get vision, you have to get with the One who gives vision.

"Now don't get me wrong, this doesn't happen overnight. Fulfilling dreams take patience, so you must learn to embrace the process. Umm hmm. You have to mature. God is more concerned with your transformation than anything else. He desires for you to look like Him."

Chloe couldn't stop the tears from flowing. Shane noticed and signaled an usher for tissues and handed them to her, squeezing her hand for comfort.

"Resentment kills dreams . . ."

Chloe bawled after that statement, because in that moment the Holy Spirit revealed to her that she was still harboring resentment toward Rico and Raegan. Rico wasn't there for her to lash out, but Raegan had made herself available to be on the receiving end of her fury by coming into her life again. Though she wished she could just move on, it was tough for her and she was unsure why.

But she knew that to get back to the place in her spiritual walk with God where she needed to be, she had to truly forgive and let it go. She'd tried that and thought she'd done that, but the mere mention of Raegan's name made her cringe.

When it was time for the altar call and the doors of the church were open for those wanting salvation and prayer, Chloe made her way forward and knelt, weeping, with Shane on his knees next to her, rubbing her back and praying for her.

"Lord, I surrender. No longer do I want to be consumed or controlled by this situation. I want to be free. I want closeness with You far greater than I've had before. I want to dream again. I need to dream again. I want to be where You want me to be," Chloe prayed between sobs.

After prayer, she accepted more tissues to wipe the tears from her face and the leakage from her nose. She was a mess, but one thing was for sure, she would never be the same. She meant every word of her prayer. She would no longer be bound by her feelings for Rico and Raegan's affair. She was done. She wanted the life that God had for her, and she wasn't planning on allowing someone else's mess to cloud her vision any longer.

When the service ended and they were back in Shane's truck, he started the engine and turned to face her.

"Is everything all right? Do you need to talk?"

"Well, it's nothing I haven't shared with you before."

"While that may be true, I've never seen you like that. We can talk about it if you want."

"That sermon touched me and made me realize that I have resentment in my heart toward Raegan and her participation in Rico's adultery, and it's interfering in my relationship with God. I can't have that. So today I left it at the altar," she answered truthfully. She had hesitated to put it into words, but something about professing it out loud to Shane and to herself solidified her choice to move forward.

"Amen to that. Thank you for allowing yourself to be vulnerable with me. I know that isn't always easy."

"It isn't, but thank you for being understanding and not judging me. I know I've had a lot to deal with for the past couple of years, and that has somehow become a weight for you as well."

"I do love you, so it's second nature. If I can't be here for you, then you wouldn't have a need for me in your life. I want forever with you, remember?" Shane said and winked.

"Yeah, I do remember you saying something like that. Thank you. I appreciate you being here for me."

"That's what heroes do!" Shane said, puffing out his chest.

Chloe laughed at his gesture and said, "Okay, no more superhero movies for you. You're cut off!"

"That's fine until the next movie is released, but for now, let's get something to eat. I'm starved."

Chloe agreed and gave him a peck on the cheek before she relaxed back in her seat so that he could drive them to their destination. As he drove, she stole glances at him. She didn't want to seem like she was being weird, but she was glad to have him in her life. Sure, she had her sister Kelly and could always talk to her, but it was different with Shane. Today was truly a new beginning for her, and she could say without a shadow of a doubt that she was ready to move forward in life and with him.

Chapter 36

Life hadn't been anything near what Shane considered normal since he became a detective. Sunday dinner with Chloe had to be cut short once again when he received a call from lead detective Morris. Another homicide called his attention away from his love.

"I'm sorry Coco. I'm on call this weekend and that was Morris," Shane apologized after he ended the call. He placed the phone screen-down on the table and reached for her hands. "I don't know if it will always be this crazy, but I hate having my time with you interrupted. I'll make it up to you later. Promise."

"I understand. Duty calls." Chloe was disappointed, but it was the life she pushed for with him being off the streets and behind the desk—only rarely was he behind the desk. It seemed he was always investigating something, taking statements, and following up on a lead. Work never seemed to end.

"If it isn't too late, I'll give you a ring when we wrap up," Shane explained, signaling the waiter for to-go boxes and the check. He didn't waste any time paying for the food, getting back to his truck, and dropping her off at her apartment. He kissed her good-bye at her door and hustled back to his truck to get home so that he could get his unmarked vehicle.

Chloe shimmied out of her church clothes and into a pair of yoga pants and a tank top. She plopped down onto the sofa and flipped through channels, pausing at a breaking news story that seemed to be covered by every local station. She'd passed it up on the first four channels, but then decided to stop briefly to see what was going on. She generally stayed away from watching the news since they hardly ever reported on anything good. She often witnessed bad news firsthand in her line of work. She chose not to watch it on TV as well if she could avoid it.

Woman falls to her death from club rooftop, the breaking news was captioned. Chloe had only heard a few of the reporter's words before turning off the TV. That was too horrific to even listen to, let alone watch as people stood around with their cell phones in the background taking pictures before the police arrived and ushered them away from the scene. Given her newfound hope she experienced at church that morning, she decided that visiting her parents was a much better choice.

∞

Shane's heart sank when he arrived at Club Indigo's grand opening and saw the puddle of blood staining the concrete near the covered body. The paramedics were already onsite, waiting for the police to investigate. *How on earth could something like this happen?* he wondered. Detective Morris was already in the area collecting evidence from where the woman's body lay and placing it in a plastic evidence bag. Shane slipped gloves on and joined in at Detective Morris' side.

"What do we know so far, Morris?"

"Well," he sighed and shook his head. "Not a whole lot. I spoke to two witnesses who both said that she was dancing and drinking, and the next thing they knew, they heard a scream but she was already over the edge."

"Isn't that wall a bit high for anyone to simply fall over it?"

"Right."

"I'll see if I can find more witnesses," Shane said and left Morris' side heading into the club. He took note of the floorplan before taking the elevator to the rooftop. Clear. He headed back down and walked to the rear of the building, where he found a few clubgoers huddled in circles talking about what they suspected happened. One woman sitting alone appeared to be shaken. Her hands trembled when she lifted her drink to her mouth and her eyes darted around the area as if she was afraid. *If she's this shaken up, why is she still here?* he wondered while walking over to speak with her. He introduced himself and asked her name, which she mumbled 'Melanie,' but he understood.

"I'm sure that was a terrible thing to witness. Are you all right? Did you see what happened?"

Melanie appeared to be in her late twenties, possibly early thirties. She didn't respond immediately. She rubbed her hands nervously along the red dress that barely covered her thighs. She glanced at Detective Shane McDaniels and turned her attention back to her glass, which she lifted to her lips once again—but this time it dropped to the ground. The shattering of the glass caused the circle of women standing nearby to nearly jump out of their skin. One of them announced that she was leaving because there was no way she would be able to enjoy herself anymore.

Shane had a feeling the woman knew something, so he sat with her for a moment and waited, hoping that she would share information that could help them find out what happened to the woman who fell off the roof.

Tears filled her eyes and she buried her face in her trembling hands. Shane's instinct was to comfort her in some way, but he didn't want his efforts to be misconstrued for anything more.

"Can I get you some water or a blanket?" The temperature was dropping and that sleeveless dress she had on probably contributed to her trembling if he had to guess.

"She was my friend," Melanie said finally, her voice barely above a whisper as she choked back tears. "She was in town staying with me."

Shane nodded, encouraging her to continue.

"And Nate," she said and paused, collecting her thoughts. "He was just so freaking mean to her. I think that's why she came here, to get away from him, you know?" she said, turning to Detective McDaniels. "The cursing, hitting, threatening was all too much for her. She wanted to get away from him, but she didn't know how. It was a cycle. They'd fight and he would tear her down physically and emotionally, she'd leave him, he'd apologize, and she'd go back to him. Then she'd find herself in the situation all over again. This time was supposed to be different.

"She'd been here three months pulling her life back together. New job. Committed to Christ. Back in church. Faithful to ministry. Volunteering. She wanted to be different, wanted a different life, and wanted to be a woman her son could be proud of," Melanie recalled, squeezing a fist full of tissues.

"What else can you tell me about Nate? His last name? Was he here this evening?" Shane asked gently, mindful of her fragile state, but he had a job to do. Something told him that this Nate was who he needed to be looking for to get his answers.

"Whitehouse is his last name. When Natalie revealed to me how he treated her, I told her to get out, and frankly, I didn't want to hear anything else about it. There was nothing she could have told me to make me see him different than the scumbag he was. She was too good for him. Too good. I wished she would have realized it sooner because we probably wouldn't be sitting here if she had," she said through broken sobs.

"Did you see Nate today?"

"Yes, briefly."

"Will you tell me what happened?" Shane asked, ears and hands poised to take in every ounce of information she was willing to give.

Melanie closed her eyes and relived the scene, explaining all that she could recall to Shane. "Natalie and I were standing around dancing and having drinks when he walked up and tapped her on the shoulder. When he spoke her name, she froze. She seemed terrified when she recognized the voice. She turned to look at him and he hugged her like they were lifelong friends. His smile was huge. From a stranger's perspective you would have sworn that he genuinely missed her. His smile eased her anxiety a bit, and she introduced us. He didn't say much, but he kept his arms around her and she seemed to be growing uncomfortable. That's when she excused herself to talk to him privately. I'm not sure what happened between the two of them after that, because that is the last time I saw her." She burst into tears again at the realization that she'd never see her friend again.

Detective Morris walked around the now empty rooftop trying to understand how Natalie could have fallen. He surmised that she had to have jumped or been pushed, given that she was only about five feet three inches tall and the barricade was about five feet tall. He glanced around the area and shook his head in sadness, before returning to the area where Shane and Melanie sat. Shane gestured for more tissues and Morris returned with napkins from the bar.

Shane handed the napkins to Melanie. "I'm sorry to put you through this, but if someone did something to Natalie, we'd like to find them. We can stop whenever you feel you've had too much," Shane said. Based on what he learned in training and from Morris, witnesses are able to provide more information when the incident is fresh on their mind, so he was hoping to get as much from her as he could without pushing her too hard.

"I know. I know. It's just hard to believe that she's gone so suddenly. I want to help. You'll just have to excuse the tears."

"Thank you. Do you remember what Nate was wearing?"

"A red polo-style shirt and blue jeans. He was bald. Maybe five feet ten inches. Medium build. You know, not thin and not thick either. He wore glasses. He also had a mark on his cheek. Maybe a birthmark or bruise, I'm not sure. I didn't get a long look at him."

Shane nodded to Detective Morris, indicating he was finished with his line of questioning. "If you can think of anything else, please give either of us a call. And will you give me a number to contact you in case we have more questions?" Melanie nodded and took his pen to scribble her number down on his notepad.

"Would you like a ride home?" Detective Morris asked.

"No, I'm all right. I'll get an Uber or a Lyft," she answered. They escorted her into the lobby on the first floor. Neither of them was comfortable leaving her there and decided to wait until a ride arrived.

"Was there a phone on her? Were you able to check it for an ICE contact?"

"Yeah, the coroner removed a little purse from her body. The phone was cracked, but still operational." Detective Morris had the box of evidence in the backseat of his car and went outside to retrieve the phone that was sealed in a Ziploc bag. Still using his gloves, he opened the bag and switched on the phone, locating her ICE contacts.

Detective Morris scrolled, tapped, and swiped until he located ICE. When he was back at Shane's side, he said, "All right, looks like she has two. The first looks like it's that lady you just talked to. Let's start with the other one, Caleb McKinney."

Chapter 37

"Honey, what's wrong?" Raegan asked, joining a stone-faced Caleb on the sofa. The color had drained from his face, his brows were wrinkled, and his mouth was slightly opened in shock.

Still clutching the phone in his hands, he turned to look at her and said, "Natalie is dead."

Raegan's hands covered her mouth in surprise. Tears slowly filled her eyes as she thought about Nicholas. Though he probably didn't remember Natalie, Raegan had felt that at some point they would share the fact that she adopted him as her own.

Pulling herself together, she placed her hands on his lap to comfort him and he covered her hands with his and looked at her, "My heart breaks for Nick."

"I know honey, I know. Who called to let you know?"

Caleb shook his head in disbelief before he responded, "She had me listed as an emergency contact. That was a detective from the Nashville Metro Police Department. Morris, I think that's what he said his name was, I'm not sure. I can't even begin to think what was going on with her or why she would be in Nashville. I don't remember her having any family there."

Raegan slid closer and wrapped her arm across the expanse of his back and placed her head on his shoulders. "I'm sorry babe."

"Yea, me too. You know a part of me was still holding a little grudge against her because she kept Nick away from me. I can never get that time back."

"But you have as much time as God will allow with him now, so you have to focus on the positive. We'll never know her reasons, but you'll have to let it go. She's gone. But maybe you should find out when the funeral will be so that we can all go."

"Are you sure you want to do that?"

Raegan nodded. She wasn't fond of the idea of traveling with the kids for the sole purpose of going to a funeral for someone she'd only met a couple of times. However, she thought it would be important for Caleb to get closure since he was still holding a grudge against Natalie. He could find peace and hopefully move forward and enjoy the time he had with Nicholas. Though Nicholas would probably not remember, she thought it was important that he went to his mother's funeral in case he had questions later in life. She understood what it felt like to go through a period of not knowing who you are and feeling abandoned. She didn't want the same for Nicholas, and she prayed that her love for him as a mother would be enough to pull him through if he ever had questions about who he was.

"I'll find out the details and we'll make arrangements to say good-bye."

"Babe, how do you feel about letting Cynthia keep an eye on the twins while the rest of us go to the service?" she asked. Though she'd only known Cynthia a short time, she felt okay leaving them with her for a couple of hours, and they seemed comfortable with Cynthia when she came to Houston for Nicholas' party.

"That sounds like a really good idea. Call her now, and we can finalize plans once we know the details."

Raegan made the call, hoping that Cynthia was available. Without hesitation, Cynthia excitedly agreed and Raegan visibly relaxed.

∞

Nicholas sat content in the middle seat of the airplane with headphones and a tablet opened to the YouTube Kids app. His love for baby shark was sure to keep him busy for at least the next hour.

The twins, on the other hand, were very interested in everyone else on the plane, standing in their parents' laps, waving and getting excited when other passengers entertained them. The bouncing and jumping lasted most of the ride, with the two of them only calming down for pretzels and juice boxes. Baby shark and their favorite toys seemed much less exciting than normal, and they preferred the crowd.

Raegan breathed a sigh of relief when the captain announced they would be landing in the next fifteen minutes. Her thighs couldn't take any more of baby girl's feet in her lap. Though the funeral was scheduled to be relatively short since Natalie didn't have any family around, Raegan was thankful she could drop the toddlers off with Cynthia for a while. As active as they were right now, a funeral was no place for the twins.

She was thankful she had enough sense to pack extra clothes. After being tugged on and splattered in juice stains, her shirt wouldn't be okay to wear anywhere.

Securing the rental car and buckling the children into the car seats, they input Cynthia Harrison's address into the GPS to drop the twins off for a few hours. Though Raegan was relieved and thankful that Cynthia agreed to watch them upon short notice, she couldn't help but feel knots forming in the pit of her stomach.

There was no room in the driveway, so Caleb pulled alongside the curb in front of the Harrisons' house. The knot in Raegan's stomach grew tighter when Caleb turned off the engine and began gathering the children to go inside. She didn't want Caleb to worry, so she didn't mention it but moved alongside him, unbuckling baby girl and grabbing their day bag.

They walked up the brick-lined path to the front door. When Nicholas noticed the white porch swing, he moved ahead so that he could swing on it a couple of times. When Raegan and Caleb arrived at the front door, Raegan rang the doorbell while trying to keep a close hold on Cassie, who wanted to join Nicholas on the swing.

"Come on Nick, we're not playing on the swing right now. Let's go inside," Caleb instructed, noticing Caleb Jr. was itching to play alongside Nicholas.

Raegan's attention was on Nicholas until the door opened without a greeting. That solidified that knot in the pit of her stomach.

Chloe stood in the doorway. No smile. No frown. She simply stood there. She was clearly not expecting to see them. She blinked a few times, her eyes roaming from the children to Caleb and back to Raegan again. Until that moment, Raegan hadn't paid much attention to how much Chloe favored Cynthia. They both stood about five feet, five inches tall, slender, perfectly arched eyebrows, light brown eyes, rounded nose, and high cheekbones.

Chloe finally stepped to the side and announced, "Come on in."

Chapter 38

"Your children are beautiful," Chloe complimented as they entered the house. When Cynthia mentioned that Raegan and Caleb were on the way over with the children, a feeling of awkwardness washed over her and her instinct was to turn around and bolt out the door, even though she'd only been at her parents' house for about fifteen minutes before the announcement. But she obeyed the tugging in her spirit that wanted her to stay. She was glad she did, because it wasn't until she saw Raegan's face again that she realized that she was in a much better place. The anger and resentment she'd been feeling toward her was not as strong.

"Thanks," Caleb and Raegan said in unison. Raegan even smiled, wanting to gauge where Chloe's heart was these days. She recalled Chloe giving her medical advice and she seemed okay then, but given they were on the phone, it was hard to tell whether she was doing it out of duty or she was ready to turn over a new leaf.

Cynthia greeted them in the living room, immediately reaching for Caleb Jr. after kneeling to hug Nicholas tightly. To Raegan's surprise, Chloe asked if she could hold one of the twins.

"Um, sure." Raegan handed Cassie to her, studying the two of them. As attached as Cassie was to Raegan, Raegan was surprised that she allowed Chloe to hold her willingly. Chloe's short hair and gold-hooped earrings immediately caught her attention. Chloe's spiked haircut was different to her, given that she was used to rustling her mother's curly hair.

"Be careful. She looks like she's about to go for your earrings."

Chloe nodded and joined her mother on the couch. "Oh, I know all about that. I'm faster than she is; she just doesn't know it yet. Can you say TT?" Cassie repeated it after Chloe and melted her heart. Chloe began having a conversation with Cassie as if she was much older than a one-year-old, and it dawned on her once again that she wanted this with Shane.

"Well it looks like you all are all good here. We'll be back in a couple of hours," Raegan said, after giving them a rundown of everything in the babies' diaper bag and what to do in an emergency.

Cynthia smiled and said, "They'll be fine. Don't forget that I'm a mother as well. They're in good hands. You guys be safe."

Raegan hugged Cynthia, kissed the twins and said her good-byes, as Caleb scooped Nicholas into his arms before heading back out of the door.

"TT?" Caleb repeated when they were safely inside the car pulling away from the curb.

Raegan chuckled and said, "My thoughts exactly. I was too stunned to say anything. I guess that means she's coming around."

"Good for her. What does that mean for you? Are you coming around?"

"I don't have any problem with starting a relationship with her, but I think I'll let her make the first move. I'm pretty sure she has much more to work past than I do."

Caleb extended his right hand and covered hers. Looking at her briefly, he said, "I'm proud to call you my wife. Keep allowing God to strengthen you, babe."

"Thanks honey. You do know that I'm stronger with you beside me."

"As am I."

"Where are we going?" Nicholas' voice rang from the backseat.

"We're going to say good-bye to one of Daddy's old friends," Caleb answered. Trying to explain to a three-year-old that they were going to his mommy's funeral was not going to make any sense to him, especially since he only knew Raegan as his mother. This would be a conversation for a much later time in Nicholas' life, when they thought he was ready to hear it.

"Oh," was all Nicholas said in response, surprising both Raegan and Caleb. He usually had one hundred and one questions, but today, he was somehow content with that one answer. And Caleb was grateful because he didn't have any other answers to give. He still found it hard to believe that Natalie was dead.

Arriving at the funeral home, they noticed there were only a few cars in the parking lot. If there wasn't a sign out front that read Nashville Heritage Funeral Home, Caleb would have bet a thousand bucks that they were on the estate of some wealthy family. Lush green grass, beautiful landscaping, eight white columns lined in front of the entrance, two levels with a balcony on the second floor did not say "funeral home" to him. The atmosphere seemed bright and cheery, but maybe that was the point.

His first impression was matched by the wood floors and decorations upon entering. He turned to hear someone calling his name.

"You must be Caleb and Raegan," Melanie said, extending her hand to greet them.

"Yes. Melanie, right?" She nodded and Caleb continued, "And this is our son Nicholas."

Melanie's eyes filled with tears again when she looked at young Nicholas. She'd been crying all morning, one of the reasons she skipped the mascara, and seeing Nicholas' eyes reminded her of Natalie's.

"It's just us," she said before leading them inside. They met with the funeral director to view the body and then followed the hearse in procession to the cemetery for the graveside service. Natalie's parents, who were both only children, had both passed away and she didn't have any brothers or sisters. Melanie was her best friend and "next of kin." Melanie had chosen to keep the arrangements private with the exception of Caleb and the detectives working Natalie's case. Detectives Morris and McDaniels were planning to stop by to see if Nate would show up.

One of the associate pastors from Melanie's church eulogized Natalie. Caleb's heart broke for her. She'd been through so much pain in her life and had finally given her life to Christ. A knot formed in his throat thinking about how things ended for her, but now she was finally getting to rest with our heavenly Father; he only wished that she didn't leave so soon. At some point, he wanted Nicholas to meet and know her. Raegan's heart broke for Nicholas because he'd never get the chance to get to know Natalie; however, she vowed to be the best mother she could be to him. She was thankful that God allowed her to be in his life. The thought of his not having a mother at all broke her heart. Though she wasn't thankful for the way her adoption of Nicholas came about, she was thankful that it happened when it did, because he had her, Caleb, and the twins to love and to be loved by them.

Melanie said a few words and so did Caleb, though his words were relatively brief. There weren't multiple Bible verses being read, friends who wanted to share words, or even song selections.

Raegan did not like funerals and generally avoided them if she could. But this was one of those times that she had to put her feelings aside and be there for Caleb and Nicholas. Though Caleb would likely never admit it, he was hurting. At one point, he did love Natalie, so the fact that she was no longer here had to hurt him a little bit, although every time she asked how he was doing, he'd say fine.

Unbeknownst to them, the detectives had been standing right outside of the tent. When the service was over, they gave their condolences and reintroduced themselves to Melanie and introduced themselves to Raegan and Caleb.

"We just wanted to stop by to check in on you. How are you holding up?" Detective Shane McDaniels asked Melanie.

"I'm all right. As well as can be expected. This is Caleb and Raegan McKinney and their son, Nicholas."

Recognition flashed across Shane's features as the names registered. It didn't take long to figure out that Raegan was Chloe's Raegan. She favored Cynthia except that she was a couple inches shorter.

"It's nice to finally meet you."

"Finally?" Raegan and Caleb asked in unison.

Chapter 39

Detectives Morris and McDaniels walked with Melanie and the McKinneys to their cars. Melanie thanked the funeral director and the minister before leaving. Caleb secured Nicholas inside of the car, pressing Play on the tablet to capture his attention with Disney Jr. videos. He closed the door and stood outside of the car along with Raegan, Melanie, and the detectives.

"We haven't been able to locate Nate yet for questioning," Detective Morris started, "but we're working on it, and we'll continue to keep you updated with any information about the case."

"Thank you, Detective," Melanie said with a weak smile, dabbing at her eyes with the crumpled tissue in her hands.

Standing next to Raegan, Caleb leaned against the car with his arms folded across his chest. He turned to check on Nicholas before asking, "So exactly what information do you all have at this point?"

Detective Morris repeated the information he gave to Caleb when he called a week ago, only adding that they'd reviewed security footage from the club and saw the two of them together, but the area of the roof where Natalie went over was a camera blindspot, something the club owner vowed to have corrected since the accident. Caleb nodded and gave the detectives his information again, indicating that he wanted to be updated regarding the case. He'd hope to have some kind of answers when the time came to have a conversation with Nicholas about Natalie, and if he were being honest with himself, he needed to know what happened.

"So," Caleb cleared his throat and switched topics, directing his question to Detective Shane McDaniels, "how do you know my wife and I?"

"I'm sorry," Shane said, shaking his head to clear his thoughts. "I'm dating her sister, Chloe."

Raegan and Caleb turned to look at each other with raised eyebrows, but said nothing, and waited to hear whatever else Shane was willing to share.

"Umm, Morris and Melanie, you two don't have to stick around for this. This is a bit personal. I'll catch up with you back at the precinct."

Morris escorted Melanie to her car, reminding her to call him if she needed anything before he headed back to the precinct.

At Morris' retreating back, Shane continued, "I've been praying for you and Chloe. This has been weighing heavily on her, and as you can imagine, a little difficult for her to accept."

Raegan nodded and said, "Same here. But I do believe that things will work out as they should. I believe in miracles."

Raegan thought about the interaction with Chloe before coming to this funeral. If that wasn't a miracle, she wasn't sure what was. Coming from a place of being ready to pounce on her to welcoming her children had to be nothing short of a miracle.

"All will be well. I trust God." Exhaling deeply, Shane asked, "So how long are you all in town? Are you planning to see the Harrisons while you're here?"

"Actually we saw them before coming here," Raegan answered.

Shane raised questioning brows.

"All was well. We're headed back there now to pick up the twins," Caleb said, checking his watch.

"Don't let me hold you. Maybe I'll get a chance to catch up with you all again before you leave, but I gotta run. I'm on duty, so I'm headed back to the precinct to work on this case. I'll be in touch," Shane said, sealing his good-bye with a handshake to both Caleb and Raegan.

Caleb walked Raegan to the passenger side and opened her door. Satisfied she was securely inside and buckled, he returned to the driver's seat, turned to her, and asked, "How many more surprises can you take?"

"I don't know babe, I don't know," she said with a chuckle. She couldn't help but wonder exactly how small was the world? She found herself excited for Chloe after meeting Shane. Though she didn't know much about him, she was certain he loved Chloe. There was no mistaking the love and adoration he had for Chloe while talking about her. Even after everything that she'd gone through with Rico, Chloe received sunshine after her storm, Shane.

∞

Raegan and Caleb had agreed to join the Harrisons for dinner after the funeral service. Chloe gave her apologies, but wasn't able to stay for dinner. Any other time, Raegan and Cynthia would have believed she was making excuses so that she wouldn't have to be in the same room with Raegan, but she seemed sincere, stating that she'd already made plans with Shane for later that evening.

After dinner, Raegan and Cynthia decided against dessert and went into the living room to drink tea, leaving the children and husbands in the kitchen. "Looks like Chloe is coming around," Cynthia said to Raegan, peering over her cup of tea.

"Seems that way. She was kind today, seemed really different," Raegan agreed. She'd been steeping her teabag in the mug of hot water for the last fifteen minutes, not having taken one sip. "I have to admit that it's hard to gauge where she is. I'd like to at least talk to her, but I'm not sure if she's going to bite my head off or welcome the interaction. I'm not saying that we have to be best friends, but we could be cordial. I know seeing me brings up memories she'd prefer to forget. And quite frankly, seeing her does the same thing for me, but I've stuffed those memories in the deep recesses of my mind."

Cynthia placed her mug on the coffee table and turned to Raegan. "Don't beat yourself up over anything that's going on with Chloe. My dear, we all have choices to make. She'll have to decide how open she allows her heart to be. But don't worry, I have a feeling that God is working on her."

"What do you mean?"

"She loves Shane, and in order to fully embrace that love, she'll have to come to terms with you, whether she wants to or not. She can't harbor hate and love at once. She'll go crazy."

"I guess you're right about that."

"Yeah, I'm right most of the time."

David Harrison entered the room, along with Caleb, Nicholas, and the twins. Judging from the looks on their faces and the remnants of crumbs on their shirts, they had indulged in Cynthia's German chocolate cake.

"Well, was it good?"

"What?" David asked, making himself comfortable in the oversized recliner adjacent to the sofa where Raegan and Cynthia sat.

"Yes, ma'am. It was delicious. The little ones all wanted seconds." Caleb took the open seat next to Raegan.

"Oh, I'll pack them some to go. They can eat it later," Cynthia suggested, rising from her seat to cut cake and wrap it for them.

"We shouldn't let her do that. I love cake and I'll end up being the one who eats it all," Raegan said to Caleb. "Just a little please Cynthia," she called to her in the kitchen.

Raegan began gathering the children's bags so that they could prepare to leave. They had an early flight the next day. Caleb ran to put them away in the rental and returned for the children.

"Here you go, Caleb. Raegan, I know how much you love cake so there's enough for you, too. Enjoy."

"Thank you so much for your hospitality. You rescued us when you watched the kids today. We appreciate it."

Cynthia dismissed her comment with the wave of her hand and pulled Raegan into her arms, squeezing her tightly. Every moment she got, she embraced her firmly, hoping that Raegan could feel the expression of her love for her.

"Anytime you're in Nashville or if you ever just want to come for a visit, all you have to do is call. You're always welcome here."

"That's right," David agreed, sliding to the edge of the recliner to rise and hug her and the children and shake Caleb's hand. "Always welcomed here. Take care and let us know when you arrive safely back in Houston."

David and Cynthia walked them to the door and watched as they got situated in the car and pulled away. David wrapped one arm around Cynthia's shoulders, squeezed her closer to him, and kissed her cheek. "Everything is going to be all right."

"Yeah, you're right," Cynthia agreed. Tears of gratefulness erupted from her eyes when she thought about how God and David looked past her faults and decided to love her anyway. God even allowed her to meet and get to know her daughter after all this time. She couldn't be more thankful.

Chapter 40

As planned, Shane visited Chloe after her shift ended. But when he rang her doorbell, he didn't seem like himself. The handsome smile accompanied by the peaceful and energetic demeanor was replaced with sadness. He offered a weak smile when she greeted him at the door, but the strength of his arms wrapped around her remained the same as always.

"What's wrong?"

"Work. Stress."

"I'm sorry. Do you want to talk about it?" Chloe stepped out of his embrace and motioned to let him into her apartment. "C'mon. This is a safe place. Dinner can wait a few minutes."

Shane accepted the invitation and walked over to the reclining sofa, which appeared to be the focus of the room. Though an essential piece of furniture, it would be better suited in a room at least twice the size. Chloe joined him, folding her legs under before sitting down.

Shane looked at Chloe and smiled. Her bright eyes were warm and engaging, inviting him to share the secrets of his soul. He could get lost in those eyes forever. Where should he begin?

Shane exhaled sharply and took one of Chloe's hands in his. "This homicide investigating is wearing me out. I know I've shared this with you before on multiple occasions, but it's draining and too depressing. But there was the most need in homicide investigations and that's where I got picked up first. Word on the street is that an opening is coming up in property crime investigations, and I think I'd much rather deal with that."

Chloe nodded, not offering any advice. She had the distinct impression that he simply needed to talk, so she allowed him to do so without interruption.

"You know in training, they teach us investigative techniques and to push to get as much information as we can from witnesses at the scene of the crime, because as time goes on they are less likely to remember all the details. Can you imagine how difficult that is? I mean, most people are still in shock. Not to mention if the witness has a personal relationship to the victim, it's traumatic for them. Obviously you have to use your judgment and handle the situation with care, but it's too much. As a person, I want to console the witness, not grill them for information. But it's the job.

"And one of the cases I'm working on now has been the most interesting yet." Shane paused and gazed into her eyes again for several seconds. He contemplated how to share that he'd met Raegan and Caleb, without sharing too much detail about the ongoing investigation of Natalie's homicide case.

"Let's just say that I met your sister."

Chloe's eyebrows bunched in confusion, while her eyes encouraged him to proceed.

"Her husband knew the victim of a case I'm working, and they were in town for the funeral. She mentioned she saw you."

"Yeah, I saw them and had the chance to meet their children. The twins are adorable," Chloe said wistfully, a smile forming on her lips.

Shane wasn't quite sure of what her reaction would be when he brought up Raegan given the difficult time she'd been having coming to terms with the situation, but a smile like that wasn't on the list. That put him on high alert. For one, he was thankful that there wasn't a scowl or hint of frustration in her features or voice, which meant that she had in fact grown past her issues. Second, she was swooning over children, which made his heart leap for joy. Suddenly, his work woes didn't matter, and he wanted to strike while the iron was hot.

"Whoa," he sang. "What is that about?" He was no longer hunched over clasping his hands. It was his turn to move and face her. He slid off the couch and perched onto the coffee table in front of her.

"I don't know what you mean."

"Oh yes you do! Your face lit up talking about the twins, and when I mentioned her name, you didn't frown like you've done a thousand times before."

"God has been answering my prayers about this situation. The more I study the Bible and the verses about forgiveness, I know I must be forgiving when God has forgiven me," she answered. She shrugged her shoulders and added, "Am I ready to be her BFF, no, but I am doing my best to follow God's Word."

"Hallelujah!"

"The highest praise, huh?"

"Indeed! Woman, I thought I would be spending the rest of your life helping you get past that. You don't know how much I've prayed for you and how relieved and thankful I am to hear and witness your deliverance. I'm serious," Shane said, willing himself next to her again and pulling her onto his lap. "Your breakthrough means as much to me as it does to you."

"How did I end up with a man who cares about all of me? My heart, mind, body, and spirit?" With the palm of her hands, she drew his face closer to hers and caressed his lips with the gentlest kiss. Pulling away, she began stroking the back of his neck and continued, "Because God loves me and I thank Him daily for loving me through you. I love you, Detective Shane McDaniels, and I support you. Even though work may be tough right now, remember that no matter what, you have my love."

"That is exactly what keeps me going. I love you, Chloe Harrison." His profession of love came freely and as one that he could shout to the world. "And now knowing that you want to have my children is definitely going to keep me going. I have to get tapped for the property crimes division or become a private detective or something so I won't bring this stress home to my family," Shane half-joked.

"Wait, wait, wait." Chloe held up both palms. "I said nothing about having your children."

"Oh but that look on your face said it for you when you mentioned the twins. So are you now telling me that you don't want to have my babies?" Shane feigned heartbreak.

"I'm not saying that I don't; I'm saying I didn't say it."

"Well, do you?" Shane's eyes filled with hope and sincerity.

"I do."

"Then it's settled. Mission number two."

"What is mission number one?"

"To make you my wife," Shane answered, returning her kiss from moments earlier. Something about hearing her say that she wanted to bear his children made him feel as if he could walk through walls. He felt invincible. If he'd been asked to lift a car right now, he believed he could do it. His confidence soared knowing that her heart was in the perfect place to accept his proposal. It was time.

Chapter 41

Shane would have welcomed the idea of not sitting behind his desk filling out paperwork today. Instead, the past two days had been relatively quiet where he and Detective Morris were concerned, and that left him alone with thoughts of his upcoming proposal. He couldn't focus enough on work to save his life. He found himself constantly walking to the coffee bar or mindlessly clicking around his computer screen. They hadn't made much headway in Natalie's case. That bothered him because that case had become slightly personal now, given Chloe's biological relationship to Raegan. He'd become emotionally entangled, but that was starting to be true for all of his cases, a very good reason he needed to move to the property crimes division ASAP. He enjoyed the investigation, but he would prefer to leave his work at work and not have it haunt his dreams as his current cases were doing.

"McDaniels, are you all right over there man?" Detective Morris called out to him. Morris' desk was ten feet away, so he easily noticed Shane's incessant tapping of the pencil on the desk.

Shane cleared his throat and answered, "Yeah, I'm cool. What's up?" The tapping stopped when he directed his attention to Morris.

"Are you wrapping up the notes on the Seymour case?"

"I'm e-mailing them to you right now. Thought about what you want to do for lunch today?"

"Nah, you can pick today. I'll go with the flow. Sure you haven't filled up enough on coffee and donuts?" Morris asked, nodding his head toward Shane's third round of donuts, which was highly unlike him. If he'd eat any, it was usually a one and done. Everyone knew he took a healthy eating approach, but that hadn't been the case today. "You sure you all right man?"

"Yeah, I'm straight."

"I think you've been in this line of work long enough to know that when something is eating at a person internally, it manifests itself externally. You've been out of your seat about ten times in the last two hours. You've eaten at least five donuts. You've been wiggling that pencil around but haven't written anything. You're loading up on coffee. You've stretched at least fifty times. So what gives? Work or woman?" Morris leaned back in his seat and folded his arms across his chest, satisfied with his assessment, and waited for Shane to respond.

"Clearly I'm the only one working this morning," Shane said, tossing a stress ball to Morris.

"That's exactly what you're not doing. What's up, man? How can I help?" Morris spoke in a quiet tone. There were a few other detectives in the room, but they were out of earshot and Morris wanted to keep their conversation private.

Shane stretched again before saying, "You know how stressful this is; I don't have to tell you that. You've been doing this for what, ten years? I'm learning the ropes, so I'll manage." Shane's insides quivered as he thought about the real reason for his jitters, Chloe. He wasn't concerned with what her answer would be, but his thoughts lingered around the how. He wanted this proposal to be just as special and memorable as he planned to make the rest of their lives. He believed she deserved more than just the four words, but something that would sweep her off her feet. He'd been rehearsing it in his mind all week, and now that tonight was the night, his nerves were getting the best of him.

"Yeah, right," Morris stretched the word, emphasizing the fact that he didn't completely believe that Shane's behavior was all about work.

Beep, beep, beep. Morris concluded his conversation with Shane when an alert came through his computer. He slid back behind his screen to check it out. The text in the e-mail read, "Sorry I didn't come forward sooner, but I now feel like this is the right thing to do." Morris hit Play on the video and watched it through the end. The video opened with a group of friends singing about piña coladas while holding one in each hand. In the background was clear footage of two people arguing—Natalie and Nate. His six-foot frame towered over her five feet four inches. Because of the singing, it was difficult to understand what was being said, but with her hands flinging around and her constantly jerking away from his grasp, the exchanged words were certainly not pleasantries. In an instant, his anger got the best of him. He grabbed her shoulders, shouting obscenities, and could now be heard over the singing. One moment they were tussling and the next she was climbing over a table trying to get away from him. He pulled her back into his arms, while she bucked and jerked in attempt to maneuver out of his grasp. The next moment her body went over the rooftop. The video ended abruptly.

Morris banged his fist on the desk.

"What's up?" The pound grabbed Shane's attention.

"Nate is our guy. I'm putting out an APB right after I send you this video. I'll go ahead and request a warrant for his arrest, too."

Shane inwardly cringed at the video playback, reminded of one of the reasons he chose to become a cop. In fourth grade, one of his classmates lost a parent to a senseless shooting. Jared's father had been jogging in the park like he did every morning at 5 a.m. when a stray bullet pierced his heart. The cops never found the person responsible and Jared had a really tough time in school for the next couple of years. He wished there was something he could do to help Jared at the time, but he couldn't help him get justice or bring his father back to life. It was at that time that he vowed he would work to help others like Jared get the justice they deserved and help families get closure. That was exactly what he planned to do in this case.

"Let's follow up with Melanie, and from her place we can head to lunch," Morris suggested after calling to make sure she was home.

Shane welcomed the opportunity to divert his thoughts, hoping they could wrap up the case and give Natalie's loved ones some closure. In the ten feet it took for Morris to reach Shane's desk, Shane was out of his seat with his jacket on and joining Morris' stride out of the precinct.

The pleasant dip in temperature jolted Shane's senses that crisp fall morning. He shoved his hands in his pockets and walked silently with Morris among the fleet of marked Ford Explorers and Dodge Chargers to Morris' unmarked Dodge Charger. As usual, Shane hopped into the passenger side, buckled up, and waited for Morris to start the engine. Starting the car was usually followed by a joke, but today Morris jumped straight into conversation about their case, asking Shane's opinions here and there, and sharing similar experiences he'd faced.

Shane noticed that Morris didn't enter Melanie's address into the GPS, but he drove the route from memory, which was odd considering he used GPS for almost everything. Shane didn't mention it, but picked up on cues about his demeanor. As Shane thought about it, Morris could have easily given Melanie the information over the phone. There was no real need to visit her again, something Shane mentioned along the route, but received pushback from Morris because he believed they should remain personable since she was grieving and alone. Morris' mother was a counselor and he'd heard too many stories about the downward spiral of grieving people who didn't have anyone to talk to or lean on during their time of bereavement. No matter how much Morris tried to convince Shane, he wasn't fooled. Morris was attracted to Melanie and this was an excuse to see her again.

Though the driveway was empty, Morris parked alongside the curb in front of Melanie's house and cut the engine. In a few short strides, he and Shane were at her front door ringing the doorbell. Melanie opened the door dressed in a pair of stone-washed denim jeans and a long-sleeve green tee.

She looked comfortable and appeared more confident and relaxed than the half-dressed fragile woman they met at the crime scene.

After seeing her again at the funeral, Morris took notice of her, and seeing her now stirred something within him. Perhaps he was supposed to be in her life in some way. Something within him hoped that when the case closed, it wouldn't also be closure for them as well. He shook his head to rid himself of the thoughts and to focus on the task at hand.

His words faltered and he extended his hand. "Um, hey. I mean, may we come in for a moment?"

"Sure, please come on in." Melanie stepped to the side to allow them inside, closing the door behind them and escorting them to the living room, where she offered soda or water, which they both declined. "So tell me, what've you got?"

Shane nodded to Morris, allowing him to lead.

"We received some anonymous video footage this morning that confirms Nate is responsible for Natalie's death. It's disturbing, so I won't show it to you unless you want to see it." He paused to give her a moment to consider whether or not she wanted to see the video feed.

"I think I'll pass for now. Has he been arrested and charged?"

"We've put out an APB and issued an arrest warrant. He wasn't found at his last known address, but we're looking for him. I'll make contact when he's in custody."

"Again, we're sorry for your loss, ma'am," Shane added.

"Thank you both for all you've done to help. I'm not sure if you always work closely with families and support them the way you've done for me, but I'm glad that I had the two of you working on Natalie's case. Thank you."

Morris stood to leave and Shane followed suit.

"I'm glad that we were able to help. You have my number, I mean our numbers; don't hesitate to call if you need anything else."

"I won't. Thank you again Detective Morris and Detective McDaniels." Melanie shook Shane's hand, followed by Morris'. She couldn't quite put her finger on it, but there was something much different about his handshake than Shane's. Was it softer? Did he linger a moment longer? She wasn't sure, but something about it definitely made her think he didn't want to let go. After escorting them out, she pondered it for a moment and waved it off. *Oh, he's just doing his job.*

"'You have my number'? Really Morris? What was that about?"

"Just facts man, just facts." He went over with the intent of asking her if he could call her when the case was over, but chickened out. He wasn't sure if it was fear or the fact that McDaniels was alongside him, but the words wouldn't come out. Instead the 'you have my number' line came out. They didn't meet each other under the most pleasant circumstances, and he didn't want to take advantage of her grief. He surmised that the timing wasn't right and he'd have to pray that he received another opportunity to see her again.

Chapter 42

"Happy birthday to you,

Happy birthday to you,

Happy birthday to the one who has my heart,

Happy birthday to you," Shane sang when Chloe opened the door. He stood in her doorway dressed in an all-black suit complemented by a red tie, holding a single red rose.

"How did I not know you could sing like that?" Chloe asked, a smile spread across her face. She could hardly contain her enthusiasm.

"It's not something that many people know about me. I tend to keep it to myself."

"Well I am impressed. Thank you, hon." She accepted the rose and stepped into his arms. "It's so good to see you. I've been missing you all week, especially since we had to cancel our last date."

"I know. I hope I can make up for it tonight if you'll let me."

"I'm not dressed all fancy for nothing. Of course I'm going to let you," Chloe purred against his lips. Chloe's off-the-shoulder bell sleeve black dress complemented his ensemble.

She paired the dress with peep toe pumps. She stepped out of his arms and spun around showing off her look.

"And that you are. I love you, Chloe, and starting now, I'm going to do everything in my power to make this your best birthday yet."

"I'm so ready." Grabbing her clutch, she turned off all the lights but the living room lamp and accompanied Shane out to his truck.

"So where are we going?" Chloe asked after they were secured inside.

"How many times do I have to say it's a surprise? It wouldn't be a surprise if I told you. Besides, you only have a few more minutes to wait."

"But what if I hate the place we're going and I can prevent you from ruining our evening?"

Shane chuckled and glanced at her before turning his attention back to the road. "I highly doubt you'd hate it. It's a surprise, but I'm not crazy enough to get too risky on a special night like this one. Birthdays are special, a gift from God, and if nothing else, I want you to always look back on your birthdays and remember that I did my part in making sure you enjoyed your special day."

"You got me there. I'll be patient. So how are your mom and dad?"

"Good. Not much to complain about. Speaking of them, Mom wants us to come over for Sunday dinner after church tomorrow. With everything going on, I completely forgot to mention it to you. Does that work for you?"

"Oh that's fine. We're always hanging out with my parents; it would be refreshing to hang out with yours for a change."

Shane nodded. "I'll let her know we'll be there."

Chloe began paying more attention to the route they were driving, trying to guess where they were headed. So much for being patient. She felt like her six-year-old self on the night before Christmas, sneaking around and shaking boxes. She made a special effort to enjoy all of her birthdays, but this one seemed different. She was more excited than usual and she didn't know whether it was because her life was different or if it was because of Shane. Whatever the case, she planned to enjoy every moment of it, maybe even the rest of the month. In a few weeks, the holiday season would kick off and her focus would shift back to everyone else.

Unbeknownst to her, Shane intentionally took a different route so that she wouldn't figure out where they were going. She racked her brain the entire time and didn't figure it out until it was obvious because they were pulling into a parking space at the Country Music Hall of Fame Museum. It was there that they shared their first kiss as adults two summers ago.

"What's going on here tonight?" Chloe asked, curiosity bubbling within her.

"Your birthday."

That wasn't the answer she was looking for, but she decided to go with it. She tried to maintain her composure and excitement as they walked the distance from Shane's truck to the entrance, her stride at a slightly faster pace than his. The dip in temperature normally would be cause for a distraction, but not today. She was completely focused on her surroundings. Confusion clouded her features when he continued to lead her through the museum, bypassing galleries and the museum store. When they reached the tree-lined outdoor courtyard, her eyes widened in surprise.

She turned to Shane and asked, "Is this for me?" halting him from entering the area.

"Happy birthday, Coco," he whispered in her ear and kissed her cheek.

Tears welled in her eyes as she took it all in. All of their parents were in attendance, along with her sister's family, and mutual friends all dressed in her favorite colors: black, green, and purple. Her vision blurred from the tears, but that didn't stop her from taking note of the table filled with gifts, decorated with number balloons three and five, and the huge table spread with some of her favorite foods. However, she didn't see a cake, and that is what she looked forward to the most when going to any party. She knew Shane was aware of that, but she didn't mention it; instead she focused on the beauty of her surroundings: the lighted trees, tea light candles that adorned the tables, and her favorite music playing softly over the speakers. Lounge sofas with a view overlooking downtown Nashville made the environment feel more personal.

Chloe and Shane made their rounds greeting their guests and thanking them for attending. When they made it to Kelly, Chloe swatted her arm and said, "As much as you like to talk about everything, you couldn't tell me or even give me a hint about this."

"I was sworn to secrecy, but there were hints along the way, only you were too busy to recognize them. But don't worry about that, you'll see soon enough. Enjoy your evening, big sis. Happy birthday! I love you lady."

"I love you too. Thanks for helping him. I know he couldn't have pulled this off alone."

"Actually, he did most of the work. Don't underestimate this gent. He was on my tail about making this night special for you." Kelly's smile reached her ears. Chloe thought she seemed extra giddy this evening, but attributed it to the fact that she and Mitch were enjoying an evening out without the kids.

"It is indeed special, my love," Chloe complimented Shane, who stood next to her with a hand on her back, guiding her through the courtyard.

Shane nodded and smiled. *Oh, this is only the beginning,* he thought.

After making sure she spoke to everyone and thanked them for coming to celebrate with her, she took to the dance floor, but that didn't last very long. Had she known Shane was throwing her a party, she would have worn different shoes or at least brought a pair of flats.

"Can I bring you a plate while you rest your feet?" Shane offered.

"No need, we have something for both of you," Cynthia said, handing a plate to her while David handed one to Shane. "You all know how people are with free food. You'll mess around and leave this party without a taste of anything."

"This turned out really nice," David complimented Shane.

"Thank you. As long as Chloe is happy, I'm happy."

"Good job, son." Cynthia gave a knowing wink to Shane as if they shared some sort of secret, something that didn't go unnoticed by Chloe. The party was indeed nice, but she wasn't sure why her mother and sister were acting goofy all of a sudden.

"Happy birthday to you . . ." Shane's parents began the serenade as they made their way through the courtyard with Chloe's cake. Guests joined in and followed them over to where Chloe was seated.

Chloe's eyes and smile grew wide when they placed the cake on the table in front of her. Its icing said *Happy birthday to the love of my life!* The white icing was trimmed in pink and purple roses with a trail of hearts leading to a pink bow-covered half-opened ring box. Instead of the ring being made of cake like the rest of it, it was the diamond Shane had purchased for Chloe.

"Make a wish!" a guest shouted when the birthday song ended.

"Before you make a wish, I have something to ask you." Shane slid to one knee, reached over to carefully pull the ring from the cake, and took a napkin to wipe off the icing. Clearing his throat, he began, "Chloe Harrison, you have been an important part of my life since elementary school. I've loved you since before I even understood what love is, and today, I profess my love to you and ask if you will be my wife. Will you marry me?"

Chloe eagerly nodded moments before she exclaimed, "Yes, of course!" Shane stood, pulled her into his arms, and showered her with kisses. Cheers and congratulatory remarks exploded from the crowd. Nearly everyone had a phone taking pictures or video of the special moment, including her sister. It was then that she pieced together her mother and Kelly's giddiness. They knew. She knew it was coming, but she didn't have any idea when it would happen. Tonight couldn't have been a better time—plus she wouldn't have to spend the next few days sending texts and making calls to share the news. Just about everyone she would want to know about her engagement was present tonight.

"So, are you gonna make a wish?" someone shouted from the back of the group.

With her arms still wrapped around Shane's neck, her gaze remained on his while she said, "Nope. There's nothing left to wish for, because I have everything I need right here."

Epilogue

Wishes of a Happy New Year were murmured among the crowd gathered at Freedom Church on New Year's Day for Shane and Chloe's wedding. Floral arrangements adorned the end chair of each row and a golden wedding arch adorned with white lilies was positioned front and center. *How Deeply I Need You* by Shekinah Glory played on repeat, setting the atmosphere for the occasion.

In the bridal holding suite, Kelly and Cynthia did an excellent job of making a fuss over Chloe's hair, makeup, and gown, wanting her to be perfect on her wedding day. None of that mattered to Chloe in the moment; she was just excited to finally marry the man she loved more than anything. She looked forward to her life with Shane, the man who took notice of every detail about her and stayed by her side through some of the best and worst moments of her life. For better or worse. He had that part down already.

Straightening the lily-adorned tiara, Nina, her wedding coordinator, announced, "It's time. Congratulations sweetheart and may the Lord bless you and your new husband beyond anything you could ever ask, think, or imagine." With that, Nina stepped out of the bridal suite with Cynthia and Janet, Shane's mother, and the bridesmaids following behind, waiting for their cue to walk down the aisle.

Chloe watched the ceremony from the privacy glass. She sucked her bottom lip between her teeth to fight back the tears that welled in her eyes when she thought about the moment and how far she'd come. She took several deep breaths to calm herself and keep her emotions in check. Minutes later, Shane entered the sanctuary with his best man. Her face brightened when she saw him standing there dressed in his black tux and purple cummerbund. Suddenly nothing else mattered. Memories of how he'd shown his love to be true over the last couple of years flashed through her mind. A few years ago when she answered Rico's phone and Raegan was on the line, she would have laughed heartily had she known this was where her life was headed, full of love and joy, the kind that God wanted her to have.

When she walked down the aisle, she noticed no one but Shane. All that mattered in that moment was getting to the man at the end of the aisle. The camera flashing, the murmurs about her dress, or the cell phones that lingered over the pews to snap her picture didn't matter. Her father whispered, "I love you and I'm confident that Shane will do his best to take care of my girl. I'm proud of you. You've made me proud once again." She completely missed everything he said because her heart and mind were focused on the man she'd locked eyes with since they entered the sanctuary. She'd have to ask her dad to repeat it later, if she even remembered.

David Harrison placed Chloe's hand in Shane's, lovingly tapped Shane's shoulder, and took his seat next to Cynthia. Shane pulled Chloe into his arms and passionately kissed her. He felt lighter than usual these days with the burden of homicide cases off his shoulders, solving and closing Natalie's case, and being able to spend more time with Chloe. He was right where he needed to be and he couldn't be more thankful.

"Slow down, son. You've got the rest of your life for that," Pastor Williams said. Laughter erupted from the crowd.

"I'm sorry, Pastor, but I couldn't help myself. I only wanted to express to this beautiful bride how much her groom loves her."

"Well let's get on with it," Pastor Williams said, proceeding with the ceremony with Chloe and Shane whispering "I love you" throughout.

Chloe could not keep her emotions in check. She cried during the entire ceremony, grateful for the love she was experiencing.

"I now pronounce you man and wife. Now," Pastor Williams emphasized, "you may kiss the bride." Applause, cheers, and whistles arose from the audience as Shane and Chloe sealed their vows with a kiss.

"I feel like I've been waiting for this moment my entire life," Shane whispered into Chloe's ear as they swayed during their first dance.

"We both have, my love."

"Today, you have made me the happiest man on earth," Shane said, showering her with compliments and kisses.

"I don't have the words to express the joy in my heart right now. I could live in this moment forever."

"That would be nice, but then we'd never get to you having our babies."

"Right," Chloe sang. "I'm ready when you are."

Shane stopped moving and looked her square in the eyes, "Well let's bid these good people good-bye and get out of here. They can manage without us."

Chloe threw her head back and roared with laughter. "You're not serious are you?"

"As sure as my name is Shane McDaniels I am. Look around. They are enjoying themselves without us anyway. They probably wouldn't even realize we've taken off."

"Maybe not you, but they will soon realize that this show-stopping mermaid dress is no longer in the building."

"Show-stopping it is, my beautiful bride."

Their banter was soon interrupted with their parents and Kelly wanting to take pictures of and with them. The last photo was being snapped by the photographer and a guest with a cell phone when Chloe locked eyes with Raegan. The MC's voice boomed over the speaker to announce it was time for the garter and bouquet toss.

Raegan and Caleb inched toward the bride and groom to offer their congratulations. Chloe pulled Raegan into her arms the moment she was within reach.

"Congratulations Chloe! I am so happy for you. You deserve this."

"Thank you Raegan, and thank you for coming," Chloe said with her arms around Raegan's neck.

Pulling away, Raegan took hold of Chloe's hands. "Thank you for inviting us. There was no way we could turn down the invitation. It was a lovely ceremony, and all of this," she waved her hand, "is amazing."

"Thank you." Chloe's smile was as wide as her eyes were bright. Raegan couldn't recall ever seeing her like this before.

Shane and Caleb greeted each other and then joined at their wives' side. All of the texting and calls over the past few months, first about the kids and then about other things, was beginning to pay off. They felt more of a connection with each other and their relationship was starting to bloom. Coming to the wedding was a no-brainer for Raegan. She was honored to receive the invite, and since they had been making such progress, she looked forward to all life had in store for Chloe. More than anyone she knew, Chloe deserved happiness.

Book Club Questions

1. How well do you think Chloe handled the family situation concerning Raegan? Do you think her response was realistic? How would you have responded if you were in Chloe's shoes?

2. Cynthia, Chloe's mother, walked away from Raegan after giving birth to her in an effort to save her marriage (at least she hoped this act was one of good measure.) What affect, if any, do you think this had on Raegan? Chloe? Cynthia's marriage? Would you have made a similar choice? Why or why not?

3. Shane made the decision to become a detective, in part, because he wanted to show Chloe that he heard her concerns about his line of work. He wanted to be with her so it was an easy choice/change for him to make. Would you make career altering decisions for love or relationships? Why or why not? Do you think Shane made a good decision?

4. In several instances, Raegan is portrayed as telling half-truths or lies of omission. How would you have handled the relationships between Cynthia, Marlena, and Chloe if you were Raegan? Would you have made similar choices?

5. If you found out today that you were adopted, would you search for your birth mother? Why or why not?

6. If you pursued your birth mother as Raegan did and found out your sister was the ex-wife of the man you slept with, how would you have handled it? Walk or way? Or attempt to form a relationship? Why or why not?

7. Was Chloe's reaction to Raegan over-the-top? Do you think she should have moved past her issues sooner, considering she forgave her?

8. Marlena felt threatened when Raegan wanted to pursue a relationship with Cynthia, even though Raegan and her father, Robert, told her she had nothing to worry about. What would you have done or said differently if you were Marlena?

9. In Book 3, Cynthia painted this picture of her marriage as being strong and able to withstand trials, however she left out one important detail - Raegan. Do you think Chloe & Kelly's response was appropriate when learning they had a sister? Were they harsh in how they treated their mother and father? Did they have a right to be angry?

10. It's pretty clear that Shane is head-over-heels in love with Chloe. Was it fair to him that Chloe made him

wait so long for a commitment? Would you blame him had he decided to move on?

11. To date, this is my fifth published fiction book. Caleb has always been my favorite male character, but Shane has shown himself just as strong and loveable. Which is your favorite and why?

12. Now that we know Raegan and Chloe are sisters, can you identify any similarities in their character?

13. Cynthia stated that Chloe would eventually have to come around if she wanted to have a relationship with Shane because both love and hate couldn't dwell in Chloe's heart. Do you agree with Cynthia? Is it possible to love fully and harbor hate? Explain.

14. The first draft of Kairos 2 is complete. Can you guess who the two main characters are? (They are introduced in this book.) E-mail me and let me know who you think they are: Natasha@natashafrazier.com

Hey!

Thank you for reading Out of the Shadows! I *think* I'm closing the chapter on this series for now. It's actually sad to think about because I've grown to know and love these characters, but I think all major characters' stories have been told (or are in the process of being told in a different series). I hope you have enjoyed this series as much as I've enjoyed writing it. It's amazing how much these stories have developed since I started book one. Initially, this was only going to be a two book series, but more "what-ifs" came about as I went on, and look at where that's gotten us! I'd love to hear what you thought of this story and any other stories in this series. E-mail me, post to Amazon, Goodreads, Facebook, etc. Thank you for your support. I certainly appreciate it!